THE UNCALLED

by
Paul Laurence Dunbar

G|P

GRINDL PRESS

ISBN: 1490422943

GP

GRINDL PRESS
grindlpress.com

This book is one of numerous titles in the
STANDARD EDITION CLASSICS SERIES
available from Grindl Press.

Other Classic Literature Series and Titles from Grindl Press
grindlpress.com

SECONDARY EDUCATION EDITIONS

Heart of Darkness

Ethan Frome

Gulliver's Travels: A Voyage to Lilliput and A Voyage to Brobdingnag

Gulliver's Travels: In Four Parts

Fathers and Sons

The Red Badge of Courage

Candide, by Voltaire

The Scarlet Letter

VOCABULARY FROM THE CLASSICS SERIES

Increase Vocabulary by Reading Franz Kafka's *Metamorphosis*

Increase Vocabulary by Reading Voltaire's *Candide*

ETHNIC STUDIES SERIES

Narrative of the Life of Frederick Douglass an American Slave

My Bondage and My Freedom

The Souls of Black Folk

The Negro

Autobiography of Black Hawk

Dedicated to My Wife

CHAPTER I

I t was about six o'clock of a winter's morning. In the eastern sky faint streaks of grey had come and were succeeded by flashes of red, crimson-cloaked heralds of the coming day. It had snowed the day before, but a warm wind had sprung up during the night, and the snow had partially melted, leaving the earth showing through in ugly patches of yellow clay and sooty mud. Half despoiled of their white mantle, though with enough of it left to stand out in bold contrast to the bare places, the houses loomed up, black, dripping, and hideous. Every once in a while the wind caught the water as it trickled from the eaves, and sent it flying abroad in a chill unsparkling spray. The morning came in, cold, damp, and dismal.

At the end of a short, dirty street in the meanest part of the small Ohio town of Dexter stood a house more sagging and dilapidated in appearance than its disreputable fellows. From the foundation the walls converged to the roof, which seemed to hold its place less by virtue of nails and rafters than by faith. The whole aspect of the dwelling, if dwelling it could be called, was as if, conscious of its own meanness, it was shrinking away from its neighbours and into itself. A sickly light gleamed from one of the windows. As the dawn came into the sky, a woman came to the door and looked out. She was a slim woman, and her straggling, dusty-coloured hair hung about an unpleasant sallow face. She shaded her eyes with her hand, as if the faint light could hurt those cold, steel-grey orbs. "It's mornin'," she said to those within. "I'll have to be goin' along to git my man's breakfast: he goes to work at six o'clock, and I 'ain't got a thing cooked in the house fur him. Some o' the rest o' you'll have to stay an' lay her out." She went back in and closed the door behind her.

"La, Mis' Warren, you ain't a-goin' a'ready? Why, there's everything to be done here yit: Margar't's to be laid out, an' this house has to be put into some kind of order before the undertaker comes."

"I should like to know what else I'm a-goin' to do, Mis' Austin. Charity begins at home. My man's got to go to work, an' he's got to have his breakfast: there's cares fur the livin' as well as fur the dead, I say, an' I don't believe in tryin' to be so good to them that's gone that you furgit them that's with you."

Mrs. Austin pinched up her shrivelled face a bit more as she replied, "Well, somebody ought to stay. I know I can't, fur I've got a ter'ble big washin' waitin' fur me at home, an' it's been two nights sence I've had any sleep to speak of, watchin' here. I'm purty near broke down."

"That's jest what I've been a-sayin'," repeated Mrs. Warren. "There's cares fur the livin' as well as fur the dead; you'd ought to take care o' yoreself: first thing you know you'll be flat o' yore own back."

A few other women joined their voices in the general protest against staying. It was for all the world as if they had been anxious to see the poor woman out of the world, and, now that they knew her to be gone, had no further concern for her. All had something to do, either husbands to get off to work or labours of their own to perform.

A little woman with a weak voice finally changed the current of talk by saying, "Well, I guess I kin stay: there's some cold things at home that my man kin git, an' the childern'll git off to school by themselves. They'll all understand."

"That's right, Melissy Davis," said a hard-faced woman who had gone on about some work she was doing, without taking any notice of the clamorous deserters, "an' I'll stay with you. I guess I've got about as much work to do as any of you," she added, casting a cold glance at the women who were now wrapped up and ready to depart, "an' I wasn't so much of a friend of Margar't's as some of you, neither, but on an occasion like this I know what dooty is." And Miss Hester Prime closed her lips in a very decided fashion.

"Oh, well, some folks is so well off in money an' time that they kin afford to be liberal with a pore creature like Margar't, even ef they didn't have nothin' to do with her before she died."

Miss Prime's face grew sterner as she replied, "Margar't Brent wasn't my kind durin' life, an' that I make no bones o' sayin' here an' now; but when she got down on the bed of affliction I done what I could fur her along with the best of you; an' you, Mandy Warren,

2

that's seen me here day in an' day out, ought to be the last one to deny that. Furthermore, I didn't advise her to leave her husband, as some people did, but I did put in a word an' help her to work so's to try to keep her straight afterwards, though it ain't fur me to be a-braggin' about what I done, even to offset them that didn't do nothin'."

This parting shot told, and Mrs. Warren flared up like a wax light. "It's a wonder yore old tracts an' the help you give her didn't keep her sober sometimes."

"Ef I couldn't keep her sober, I wasn't one o' them that set an' took part with her when she was gittin' drunk."

"'Sh!'sh!" broke in Mrs. Davis: "ef I was you two I wouldn't go on that way. Margar't's dead an' gone now, an' what's past is past. Pore soul, she had a hard enough time almost to drive her to destruction; but it's all over now, an' we ought to put her away as peaceful as possible."

The women who had all been in such a hurry had waited at the prospect of an altercation, but, seeing it about to blow over, they bethought themselves of their neglected homes and husbands, and passed out behind the still irate Mrs. Warren, who paused long enough in earshot to say, "I hope that spiteful old maid'll have her hands full."

The scene within the room which the women had just left was anything but an inviting one. The place was miserably dirty. Margaret had never been a particularly neat housewife, even in her well days. The old rag carpet which disfigured the floor was worn into shreds and blotched with grease, for the chamber was cooking- and dining- as well as sleeping-room. A stove, red with rust, struggled to send forth some heat. The oily black kerosene lamp showed a sickly yellow flame through the grimy chimney.

On a pallet in one corner lay a child sleeping. On the bed, covered with a dingy sheet, lay the stark form out of which the miserable life had so lately passed.

The women opened the blinds, blew out the light, and began performing the necessary duties for the dead.

"Anyhow, let her body go clean before her Maker," said Miss Hester Prime, severely.

"Don't be too hard on the pore soul, Miss Hester," returned Mrs. Davis. "She had a hard time of it. I knowed Margar't when she wasn't so low down as in her last days."

"She oughtn't never to 'a' left her husband."

"Oh, ef you'd 'a' knowed him as I did, Miss Hester, you wouldn't never say that. He was a brute: sich beatin's as he used to give her when he was in liquor you never heerd tell of."

"That was hard, but as long as he was a husband he was a protection to her name."

"True enough. Protection is a good dish, but a beatin's a purty bitter sauce to take with it."

"I wonder what's ever become of Brent."

"Lord knows. No one 'ain't heerd hide ner hair o' him sence he went away from town. People thought that he was a-hangin' around tryin' to git a chance to kill Mag after she got her divorce from him, but all at once he packed off without sayin' a word to anybody. I guess he's drunk himself to death by this time."

When they had finished with Margaret, the women set to work to clean up the house. The city physician who had attended the dead woman in her last hours had reported the case for county burial, and the undertaker was momentarily expected.

"We'll have to git the child up an' git his pallet out of the way, so the floor kin be swept."

"A body hates to wake the pore little motherless dear."

"Perhaps, after all, the child is better off without her example."

"Yes, Miss Hester, perhaps; but a mother, after all, is a mother."

"Even sich a one as this?"

"Even sich a one as this."

Mrs. Davis bent over the child, and was about to lift him, when he stirred, opened his eyes, and sat up of his own accord. He appeared about five years of age. He might have been a handsome child, but hardship and poor feeding had taken away his infantile plumpness, and he looked old and haggard, even beneath the grime on his face. The kindly woman lifted him up and began to dress him.

"I want my mamma," said the child.

Neither of the women answered: there was something tugging at their heart-strings that killed speech.

Finally the little woman said, "I don't know ef we did right to let him sleep through it all, but then it was sich a horrible death."

When she had finished dressing the child, she led him to the bed and showed him his mother's face. He touched it with his little grimy finger, and then, as if, young as he was, the realization of his bereavement had fully come to him, he burst into tears.

Miss Hester turned her face away, but Mrs. Davis did not try to conceal her tears. She took the boy up in her arms and comforted him the best she could.

"Don't cry, Freddie," she said; "don't cry; mamma's—restin'. Ef you don't care, Miss Prime, I'll take him over home an' give him some breakfast, an' leave him with my oldest girl, Sophy. She kin stay out o' school to-day. I'll bring you back a cup o' tea, too; that is, ef you ain't afeared—"

"Afeared o' what?" exclaimed Miss Prime, turning on her.

"Well, you know, Miss Hester, bein' left alone—ah—some people air funny about—"

"I'm no fool, Melissy Davis. Take the child an' go on."

Miss Hester was glad of the chance to be sharp. It covered the weakness to which she had almost given way at sight of the child's grief. She bustled on about her work when Mrs. Davis was gone, but her brow was knit into a wrinkle of deep thought. "A mother is a mother, after all," she mused aloud, "even sich a one."

CHAPTER II

For haste, for unadulterated despatch, commend me to the county burying. The body politic is busy and has no time to waste on an inert human body. It does its duty to its own interest and to the pauper dead when the body is dropped with all celerity into the ground. The county is philosophical: it says, "Poor devil, the world was unkind to him: he'll be glad to get out of it: we'll be doing him a favour to put him at the earliest moment out of sight and sound and feeling of the things that wounded him. Then, too, the quicker the cheaper, and that will make it easier on the taxpayers." This latter is so comforting! So the order is written, the funeral is rushed through, and the county goes home to its dinner, feeling well satisfied with itself,—so potent are the consolations of philosophy at so many hundreds per year.

To this general order poor Margaret's funeral proved no exception. The morning after her decease she was shrouded and laid in her cheap pine coffin to await those last services which, in a provincial town, are the meed of saint and sinner alike. The room in which she lay was very clean,—unnaturally so,—from the attention of Miss Prime. Clean muslin curtains had been put up at the windows, and the one cracked mirror which the house possessed had been covered with white cloth. The lace-like carpet had been taken off the floor, and the boards had been scrubbed white. The little stove in the corner, now cold, was no longer red with rust. In a tumbler on a little table at Margaret's head stood the only floral offering that gave a touch of tenderness to the grim scene,—a bunch of home-grown scarlet and white geraniums. Some woman had robbed her wintered room of this bit of brightness for the memory of the dead. The perfume of the flowers mingled heavily with the faint odour which pervades the chamber of death,—an odour that is like the reminiscence of sorrow.

Like a spirit of order, with solemn face and quiet tread, Miss

6

Hester moved about the room, placing one thing here, another there, but ever doing or changing something, all with maidenly neatness. What a childish fancy this is of humanity's, tiptoeing and whispering in the presence of death, as if one by an incautious word or a hasty step might wake the sleeper from such deep repose!

The service had been set for two o'clock in the afternoon. One or two women had already come in to "sit," but by half-past one the general congregation began to arrive and to take their places. They were mostly women. The hour of the day was partially responsible for this; but then men do not go to funerals anyway, if they can help it. They do not revel, like their sisters, in the exquisite pleasure of sorrow. Most of the women had known pain and loss themselves, and came with ready sympathy, willing, nay, anxious to be moved to tears. Some of them came dragging by one hand children, dressed stiffly, uncomfortably, and ludicrously,—a medley of soiled ribbons, big collars, wide bows, and very short knickerbockers. The youngsters were mostly curious and ill-mannered, and ever and anon one had to be slapped by its mother into snivelling decorum. Mrs. Davis came in with one of her own children and leading the dead woman's boy by the hand. At this a buzz of whispered conversation began.

"Pore little dear," said one, as she settled the bow more securely under her own boy's sailor collar,—"pore little dear, he's all alone in the world."

"I never did see in all my life sich a young child look so sad," said another.

"H'm!" put in a third; "in this world pore motherless childern has plenty o' reason to look sad, I tell you."

She brushed the tears off the cheek of her little son whom she had slapped a moment before. She was tender now.

One woman bent down and whispered into her child's ear as she pointed with one cotton-gloved finger, "See, Johnny, see little Freddie, there; he 'ain't got no mother no more. Pore little Freddie! ain't you sorry fur him?" The child nodded, and gazed with open-eyed wonder at "little Freddie" as if he were of a new species.

The curtains, stirred by the blast through the loose windows, flapped dismally, and the people drew their wraps about them, for the fireless room was cold. Steadily, insistently, the hive-like drone of conversation murmured on.

"I wonder who's a-goin' to preach the funeral," asked one.

"Oh, Mr. Simpson, of the Methodist Church, of course: she used to go to that church years ago, you know, before she backslid."

"That's jest what I've allus said about people that falls from grace. You know the last state o' that man is worse than the first."

"Ah, that's true enough."

"It's a-puttin' yore hand to the ploughshare an' then turnin' back."

"I wonder what the preacher'll have to say fur her. It's a mighty hard case to preach about."

"I'm wonderin' too what he'll say, an' where he'll preach her."

"Well, it's hard to tell. You know the Methodists believe that there's'salvation to be found between the stirrup an' the ground.'"

"It's a mighty comfortin' doctern, too."

"An' then they do say that she left some dyin' testimony; though I 'ain't never heerd tell the straight of it."

"He can't preach her into heaven, o' course, after her life. Leastways it don't hardly seem like it would be right an' proper."

"Well, I don't think he kin preach her into hell, neither. After a woman has gone through all that pore Margar't has, it seems to me that the Lord ought to give her some consideration, even if men don't."

"I do declare, Seely Matthews, with yore free thinkin' an' free speakin', you're put' nigh a infidel."

"No, I ain't no infidel, neither, but I ain't one o' them that sings, 'When all thy mercies, O my God,' and thinks o' the Lord as if He was a great big cruel man."

"Well, I don't neither; but—"

"'Sh!'sh!"

The woman's declaration of principle was cut short by the entrance of the minister, the Rev. Mr. Simpson. He was a tall, gaunt man, in a coat of rusty black. His hair, of an indeterminate colour, was slightly mixed with grey. A pair of bright grey eyes looked out from underneath bushy eyebrows. His lips were close set. His bony hands were large and ungainly. The Rev. Mr. Simpson had been a carpenter before he was "called." He went immediately to the stand where lay the Bible and hymn-book. He was followed by a man who had entered with him,—a man with soft eyes and a kindly face. He was as tall as the pastor, and slender, but without the other's gauntness. He was evidently a church official of some standing.

8

With strange inappropriateness, the preacher selected and gave out the hymn:

Sister, thou wast mild and lovely, Gentle as the summer's breeze.

With some misgivings, it was carried through in the wavering treble of the women and the straggling bass of the few men: then the kindly-faced man, whom the preacher addressed as "Brother Hodges," knelt and offered prayer. The supplication was very tender and childlike. Even by the light of faith he did not seek to penetrate the veil of divine intention, nor did he throw his javelin of prayer straight against the Deity's armour of eternal reserve. He left all to God, as a child lays its burden at its father's feet, and many eyes were moist as the people rose from their knees.

The sermon was a noisy and rather inconsequential effort. The preacher had little to say, but he roared that little out in a harsh, unmusical voice accompanied by much slapping of his hands and pounding of the table. Towards the end he lowered his voice and began to play upon the feelings of his willing hearers, and when he had won his meed of sobs and tears, when he had sufficiently probed old wounds and made them bleed afresh, when he had conjured up dead sorrows from the grave, when he had obscured the sun of heavenly hope with the vapours of earthly grief, he sat down, satisfied.

The people went forward, some curiously, some with sympathy, to look their last on the miserable dead. Mrs. Davis led the weeping child forward and held him up for a last gaze on his mother's face. The poor geraniums were wiped and laid by the dead hands, and then the undertaker glided in like a stealthy, black-garmented ghost. He screwed the pine-top down, and the coffin was borne out to the hearse. He clucked to his horses, and, with Brother Hodges and the preacher in front, and Mrs. Davis, Miss Prime, and the motherless boy behind, the little funeral train moved down the street towards the graveyard, a common but pathetic spectacle.

Mrs. Warren had remained behind to attend to the house. She watched the short procession out of sight. "I guess Margar't didn't have no linen worth havin'," she said to herself, "but I'll jest look." And look she did, but without success. In disappointment and disgust she went out and took the streamer of dusty black and dingy white crape from the door where it had fluttered, and, bringing it in, laid it on the empty trestles, that the undertaker might find it when he came for them. She took the cloth off the mirror, and then, with one searching look around to see that she had missed nothing worth taking, she went out, closing and locking the door behind her.

"I guess I'm as much entitled to anything Mag had as any one else," said Mrs. Warren.

CHAPTER III

By common consent, and without the formality of publication or proclamation, the women had agreed to meet on the day after the funeral for the purpose of discussing what was best to be done with the boy Fred. From the moment that Mrs. Davis had taken charge of him, he had shown a love for her and confidence in her care that had thoroughly touched that good woman's heart. She would have liked nothing better than to keep him herself. But there were already five hungry little Davises, and any avoidable addition to the family was out of the question. To be sure, in the course of time there were two more added to the number, but that was unavoidable, and is neither here nor there. The good woman sat looking at the boy the night after his mother had been laid away. He sat upon the floor among her own children, playing in the happy forgetfulness of extreme youth. But to the mother's keen eye there was still a vague sadness in his bearing. Involuntarily, the scene and conditions were changed, and, instead of poor Margaret, she herself had passed away and was lying out there in a new-made grave in bleak and dreary Woodland. She thought how her own bairns would be as motherless and forlorn as the child before her, and yet not quite, either, for they had a father who loved them in his own quiet undemonstrative way. This should have consoled her in the sorrows she had conjured up, but, like a woman, she thought of the father helpless and lonely when she had gone, with the children huddled cheerlessly about him, and a veil of tears came between her and the youngsters on the floor. With a great rush of tenderness, she went and picked the motherless boy up and laid his head on her breast.

"Pore Freddie," she said, "I wish you could stay here all the time and play with the other little ones."

The child looked up at her with wondering eyes. "I kin stay till mamma comes back," he answered.

"But, Freddie dear, mamma won't come back any more. She's"—

the woman hesitated—"she's in heaven."

"I want my mamma to come back," moaned the child. "I don't want her to stay in heaven."

"But you mustn't cry, Freddie; an', some day, you kin go an' see mamma."

The child's curiosity got the better of his grief. He asked, "Is heaven far, Mis' Davis?"

"Yes, dear, awful far," she answered. But she was wrong. Heaven is not far from the warm heart and tender hands of a good woman.

The child's head drooped, and he drowsed in her arms.

"Put him to bed, Melissy,—pore little fellow," said her husband in husky tones. He had been listening and watching them around the edge of his paper. The child slept on, while the woman undressed him and laid him in the bed.

On the morrow the women dropped in one by one, until a half-dozen or more were there, to plan the boy's future. They were all poor, and most of them had families of their own. But all hoped that there might be some plan devised whereby Margaret's boy might find a refuge without going to the orphans' asylum, an institution which is the detestation of women. Mrs. Davis, in expressing her feelings, expressed those of all the others: "I hate so to think of the pore little feller goin' to one o' them childern's homes. The boys goin' around in them there drab clothes o' theirs allus look like pris'ners to me, an' they ain't much better off."

"An' then childern do learn so much weekedness in them places from the older ones," put in another.

"Oh, as fur that matter, he'll learn devilment soon enough anywhere," snapped Mrs. Warren, "with that owdacious father o' his before him. I wouldn't take the child by no means, though his mother an' me was friends, fur blood's bound to tell, an' with sich blood as he's got in him I don't know what he'll come to, an' I'm shore I don't want to be a-raisin' no gallus-birds."

The women felt rather relieved that Mrs. Warren so signally washed her hands of Freddie. That was one danger he had escaped. The woman in question had, as she said, been a close friend of Margaret's, and, as such, an aider in her habits of intemperance. It had been apprehended that her association with the mother might lead her to take the child.

"I'd like to take Freddie myself," Mrs. Davis began again, "but with my five, an' John out o' work half the time, another mouth to feed an' another pair o' feet to cover would mean a whole lot. Though I do think that ef I was dead an' my childern was sent to that miserable orphans' home, I'd turn over in my grave."

"It's a pity we don't know some good family that 'ain't got no childern that 'ud take him an' bring him up as their own son," said a little woman who took *The Hearthside*.

"Sich people ain't growin' on trees no place about Dexter," Mrs. Warren sniffed.

"Well, I'm sure I've read of sich things. Ef the child was in a book it 'ud happen to him, but he ain't. He's a flesh and blood youngster an' a-livin' in Dexter."

"You couldn't give us no idee what to do, could you, Mis' Austin?"

"Lord love you, Mis' Davis, I've jest been a-settin' here purty nigh a-thinkin' my head off, but I 'ain't seen a gleam of light yit. You know how I feel an' jest how glad I'd be to do something, but then my man growls about the three we've got."

"That's jest the way with my man," said the little woman who took her ideas of life from the literature in *The Hearthside*. "He allus says that pore folks oughtn't to have so many childern."

"Well, it's a blessin' that Margar't didn't have no more, fur goodness knows it's hard enough disposin' o' this one."

Just then a tap came at Mrs. Davis's door, and she opened it to admit Miss Hester Prime.

"I'm ruther late gittin' here," said the new-comer, "but I've been a-neglectin' my work so in the last couple o' days that I've had a power of it to do to-day to ketch up."

"Oh, we're so glad you've come!" said one of the women. "Mebbe you kin help us out of our fix. We're in sich a fix about little Freddie."

"We don't want to send the pore little dear to the childern's home," broke in another.

"It's sich an awful place fur young childern—"

"An' they do look so pitiful—"

"An' learn so much weekedness."

And, as is the manner of women in council, they all began talking at once, pouring into the new-comer's ears all the suggestions and objections, hopes and fears, that had been made or urged during their conference.

To it all Miss Hester listened, and there was a soft glow on her face the while; but then she had been walking, which may account for the flush. The child, all unconscious that his destiny was being settled, was playing with two of the little Davises at the other end of the room. The three days of good food, good treatment, and pleasant surroundings had told on him, and he looked less forlorn and more like the child that he was. He was clean. His brown eyes were sparkling with amusement, and his brown hair was brushed up into the damp "roach" so dear to a woman's heart. He was, thus, a far less forbidding sight than on the morning of his mother's death, when, dingy and haggard, he rose from his dirty pallet. As she listened to the varied remarks of her associates, Miss Hester allowed her eyes to wander to the child's face, and for a moment a tenderer expression grew about her lips, but in an instant it was gone, and, as if she had been near committing herself to folly, she made amends by drawing her countenance into more than its usually severe lines.

Mrs. Warren, who was always ready with a stab, and who had not forgotten her encounter of two days ago, spoke up with a little malicious laugh. "Miss Hester 'ain't got no family: mebbe she might take the child. 'Pears like she ought to be fond o' childern."

Mrs. Davis immediately came to the rescue. "We don't expect no sich thing of Miss Hester. She's never been around childern, an' don't know nothin' about takin' keer o' them; an' boys air hard to manage, anyhow."

"Oh, I should think Miss Hester could manage 'most anything," was the sneering rejoinder.

The women were aghast at such insolence. They didn't know what the effect might be on Miss Prime. They looked at her in alarm. Her cold grey eye impaled Mrs. Warren for an instant only, and then, paying no more attention to her, she said quietly, "I was thinkin' this whole matter over while I was finishin' up my work to come here, an', says I to myself, 'Now there's Melissy Davis,—she's the very one that 'ud be a mother to that child,' says I, 'an' she'd bring him up right as a child should be brought up.' I don't know no more mannerly, nice-appearin' childern in this neighbourhood, or the whole town, fur that matter, than Melissy's—'"

"Oh, Miss Hester!" faltered Mrs. Davis.

But Miss Prime went on, unheeding the interruption. "Thinks I, 'Melissy's got a houseful already, an' she can't take another.' Then you comes into my mind, Mis' Austin, an' says I, 'La me! she's got three herself, an' is young yit; she'll have her hands full to look after her own family.' Well, I thought of you all, an' some of you had families, an' some of you had to go out fur day's work; an' then there's some people's hands I wouldn't want to see the child fall into." (This with an annihilating glance in Mrs. Warren's direction.) "You know what the Bible says about the sins of the father; well, that child needs proper raisin': so in this way the Lord showed it to me that it was my dooty to take up the burden myself."

First there was an absolute silence of utter astonishment, and then, "Oh, Miss Hester!" broke from a full chorus of voices.

"You don't reelly mean it, Miss Hester?" said Mrs. Davis.

"I do that; but I want you all to understand that it ain't a matter of pleasure or desire with me; it's dooty. Ef I see a chance to save a soul from perdition an' don't take it, I am responsible, myself, to the Lord for that soul."

The women were almost too astounded to speak, Mrs. Warren not less than the rest of them. She had made her suggestion in derision, and here it was being acted upon in sober earnest. She was entirely routed.

"Now, Melissy, ef there ain't no one that disagrees with me, you might as well pack up what few things the child has, an' I'll take him along."

No one objected, and the few things were packed up. "Come, Freddie," said Mrs. Davis tremulously, "get on yore hat." The child obeyed. "You're a-goin' to be Miss Hester's little boy now. You must be good."

Miss Prime held out her hand to him, but the child drew back and held to his protectress's skirt. A hurt expression came into the spinster's face. It was as if the great sacrifice she was making was being belittled and rejected by a child. Mrs. Warren laughed openly.

"Come, Freddie, be nice now, dear; go with Miss Hester."

"I want to stay with you," cried the child.

"Pore little dear!" chorussed the women.

"But Mis' Davis can't keep the little boy; now he must go with Miss Prime, an' sometimes he kin come an' see Mis' Davis an' play with John an' Harriet. Won't that be nice?"

"I want to stay with you."

"Come, Frederick," said Miss Prime.

"Go now, like a good boy," repeated Mrs. Davis. "Here's a copper fur you; take it in yore little hand,—that's a man. Now kiss me good-bye. Kiss John an' Harriet."

The child, seeing that he must go, had given up resistance, and, doing as he was bidden, took Miss Prime's hand, sobbingly. Some of us do not learn so soon to bow to the inevitable.

"Good-bye, ladies. I must git back to my work," said Miss Hester.

"Good-bye, good-bye, Miss Hester," came the echo.

The moment the door closed behind her and her charge, there was a volley of remarks:

"Oh, I do hope she'll be good to him."

"I wonder how she'll manage him."

"Pore child, he didn't want to go at all."

"Who'd have thought it of Miss Hester?"

"I wish I could have kept him myself," said Mrs. Davis, tearfully. "It hurt my heart to see him cling to me so."

"Never you mind, Melissy Davis; you've done yore whole dooty as well as you could."

Mrs. Warren rose and put her shawl over her head preparatory to going. "As fur my part," she said, "I'd 'a' ruther seen that child in the childern's home, devilment or no devilment, than where he is. He won't dare to breathe from this hour on."

The women were silent for a moment, and then Mrs. Davis said, "Well, Miss Hester's well-meanin'."

CHAPTER IV

A t the top of the mean street on which Margaret's house was situated, and looking down upon its meaner neighbours in much the same way that its mistress looked upon the denizens of the street, stood Miss Prime's cottage. It was not on the mean street,—it would have disdained to be,—but sat exactly facing it in prim watchfulness over the unsavoury thoroughfare which ran at right angles. The cottage was one and a half stories in height, and the upper half-story had two windows in front that looked out like a pair of accusing eyes. It was painted a dull lead colour. In summer the front yard was filled with flowers, hollyhocks, bachelor's-buttons, sweet-william, and a dozen other varieties of blooms. But they were planted with such exactness and straightness that the poor flowers looked cramped and artificial and stiff as a party of angular ladies dressed in bombazine. Here was no riot nor abandon in growth. Everything had its place, and stayed therein or was plucked up.

"I jest can't abide to see flowers growin' every which way," Miss Prime used to remark, "fur all the world like a neighbourhood with different people's children traipsin' through everybody else's house. Everything in order, is my motto."

Miss Hester had nearly arrived at her fortieth mile-stone; and she effected the paradox of looking both younger and older than her age. Younger, because she had always taken excellent care of herself. Her form had still much of the roundness of youth, and her step was sprightly and firm. She looked older than her age, because of the strong lines in her face, the determined set of her lips, and the general air of knowledge and self-sufficiency which pervaded her whole being. Throughout her life she had sacrificed everything to duty, whether it was the yearning of her own heart or the feelings of those who loved her. In the world about her she saw so much of froth and frivolity that she tried to balance matters by being especially staid and stern herself. She did not consider that in the seesaw of life it takes more than one person to toss up the weight of the world's wickedness. Her existence was governed by rigid rules, from which she never departed.

It is hard to explain just what Miss Hester's position was among the denizens of the poorer quarter. She was liked and disliked, admired and feared. She would descend upon her victims with unasked counsel and undesired tracts. Her voice was a trumpet of scathing invective against their shiftlessness, their untidiness, and their immorality, but her hand was as a horn of plenty in straitened times, and her presence in sickness was a comfort. She made no pretence to being good-hearted; in fact, she resented the term as applied to herself. It was all duty with her.

Up through the now dismantled garden to the prim cottage she led the boy Fred. The child had not spoken a word since he had left the house of his friend. His little heart seemed to be suddenly chilled within him. Miss Hester had been equally silent. Her manner was constrained and embarrassed. She had, indeed, tried to find some words of soothing and encouragement to say to the child, such as she had heard Melissa Davis use; but she could not. They were not a part of her life's vocabulary. Several times she had essayed to speak, but the sentences that formed in her mind seemed so absurd and awkward that she felt them better unsaid.

It is true that every natural woman has the maternal instinct, but unless she has felt the soft face of a babe at her breast and looked down into its eyes as it drew its life from her life, she can know nothing of that freemasonry of womanhood which, by some secret means too deep and subtle for the knowledge of outsiders, wins the love of childhood. It is not so with men, because the childish mind does not demand so much of them, even though they be fathers. To be convinced, look about you and see how many more bachelors than maids are favourites with children.

Once within the house, Miss Hester was at an entire loss as to what to do with her charge. She placed him in a chair, where he sat disconsolately. She went to the bookshelves and laid her hand upon "Pilgrim's Progress;" then she reflected that Freddie was just five years old, and she allowed a smile to pass over her face. But her perplexity instantly chased the expression away. "How on airth am I a-goin' to do any work?" she asked herself. "I'm shore I can't set down an' tell that child stories all the time, as I've heerd tell o' folks doin'. What shall I do with him?" She had had a vague idea that the time of children was taken up in some way. She knew, of course, that they had to be washed and dressed, that they had to eat three times a day, and after all to sleep; but what was to be done with them in the mean time?

"Oh," sighed the poor woman, "if he was only old enough to go to school!" The wish was not entirely unmotherly, as motherhood goes in these days, for it is not an unusual thing for mothers to send their babes off to kindergarten as soon as they begin to babble, in order to be relieved of the responsibility of their care. But neither wishes nor hopes availed. It was a living, present situation with which Miss Hester had to grapple. Suddenly she bethought herself that children like pictures, and she secured from the shelf a copy of the "Bible Looking-Glass." This she opened and spread out on the child's knees. He glanced at it a moment or two, and then began to turn the leaves, his eyes riveted on the engravings. Miss Hester congratulated herself, and slipped out to work. The thought came to her, of course, that the novelty of "Bible Looking-Glasses" couldn't remain for ever, but she put the idea by in scorn. "Sufficient unto the day is the evil thereof." The book was good while it lasted. It entertained the child and gave him valuable moral lessons. This was the woman's point of view. To Fred there was no suggestion of moral lessons. It was merely a lot of very fine pictures, and when Miss Prime had gone he relaxed some of his disconsolate stiffness and entered into the contemplation of them with childish zest. His guardian, however, did not abandon her vigilance, and in a few minutes she peeped through the door from the kitchen, where she was working, to see how her charge got on. The sight which met her eyes made her nearly drop the cup which she held in her hand and with which she had been measuring out flour for a cup-cake. With the book spread out before him, Freddie was lying flat on his stomach on the floor, with his little heels contentedly kicking the air. His attitude was the expression of the acme of childish satisfaction.

Miss Prime's idea of floors was that they were to be walked on, scrubbed, measured, and carpeted; she did not remember in all the extent of her experience to have seen one used as a reading-desk before. But she withdrew without a word: the child was quiet, and that was much.

About this time, any one observing the cottage would have seen an old-fashioned phaeton, to which a plump old nag was hitched, driven up to the door and halted, and a man alight and enter at the gate. If the observer had been at Margaret's funeral, he would instantly have recognised the man as the Rev. Mr. Simpson's assistant, Mr. Hodges. The man walked deliberately around to the kitchen, and, tapping at the door, opened it without ceremony and went in, calling out, "Miss Hester, Miss Hester, I'm a-runnin' right in on you."

"I do declare, 'Liphalet Hodges, you do beat all fur droppin' in on a body at unexpected times."

"Well, I guess you're right. My comin''s a good deal like the second comin' o' the Son o' man'll be. I guess you're right."

To Miss Prime, Eliphalet Hodges was always unexpected, although he had been dropping in this way before her mother and father died, twenty years gone.

"Well, I 'low, 'Liphalet, that you've heerd the news."

"There ain't no grass grows under the feet of the talkers in this town, I tell you."

"Dear me! a body can't turn aroun' without settin' a whole forest of tongues a-waggin' every which way."

"Oh, well, Miss Hester, we got to 'low that to yore sex. The women folks must talk."

"My sex! It ain't my sex only: I know plenty o' men in this town who air bigger gossips 'n the women. I'll warrant you didn't git this piece o' news from no woman."

"Well, mebbe I didn't, but I ca'c'late there wa'n't no men there to git it fust hand."

"Oh, I'll be bound some o' the women had to go an' tell a man the fust thing: some women can't git along without the men."

"An' then, ag'in, some of 'em kin, Miss Hester; some of 'em kin."

"You'd jest as well start out an' say what you want to say without a-beatin' about the bush. I know, jest as well as I know I'm a-livin', that you've come to tell me that I was a fool fur takin' that child. 'Liphalet, don't pertend: I know it."

"Oh, no, Miss Hester; I wouldn't dast do nothin' like that; you know, 'He that calleth his brother a fool is in danger o' hell fire,' an' I 'low the Lord don't make it no easier when it happens to be a sister. No, Miss Hester, you know yore own business best, an' you've got along this fur without bein' guided by people. I guess you'll git through; but a child, Miss Hester, don't you think that it's a leetle bit resky?"

"Resky? I don't see why. The child ain't a-goin' to eat me or burn the house down."

"No, no,—none o' that,—I don't mean that at all; but then, you see, you 'ain't never had no—that is—you 'ain't had much experunce in the bringin' up o' childern, specially boys."

"Much! I 'ain't had none. But I've been brought up."

"That's true, that's true, an' a mighty good job yore mother made of it, too. I don't know of no spryer or stirrin'er woman around here at yore age."

"At my age! 'Liphalet, you do talk as ef I was about fifty."

"Well, ef I do, I ain't a sayin' what I want to say, so I'd better hush. Where is the little fellow?"

For answer, Miss Prime pushed the door open and bade him peep. Freddie was still upon the floor, absorbed in his book. The man's face lighted up: he pulled the door to long enough to say, "I tell you, Miss Hester, that boy's a-goin' to make a great reader or a speaker or somethin'. Jest look how wrapped up he is in that book."

"Well, I do hope an' pray to goodness that he'll make somethin' better than his father ever made."

"Ef he don't under yore trainin', it'll be because there ain't nothin' in him.—Come here, Freddie," called Hodges, pushing the door open, and holding out his hand with a smile. The child got up from the floor and came and put his hand in the outstretched one.

"Well, I declare!" exclaimed Miss Hester. "I tried my level best to git that child to make up with me, an' he would n't."

"It's jest like I say, Miss Hester: you 'ain't never had no experunce in raisin' childern."

"An' how many have you ever raised, 'Liphalet?"

The bachelor acknowledged defeat by a sheepish smile, and turned again to the child. "You want to go a-ridin' in my buggy, Freddie?"

"Yes, sir," said the child, unhesitatingly.

"All right; Uncle 'Liph'll take him out fur a while. Git his hat an' wrap him up, Miss Hester, so Jack Frost can't ketch him."

The man stood smiling down into the child's face: the boy, smiling back, tightened his grasp on the big hand. They were friends from that moment, Eliphalet Hodges and Fred.

They went out to the old phaeton, with Miss Prime's parting injunction ringing after them, "Don't keep that child out in the cold too long, 'Liphalet, an' bring him back here croupy."

"Oh, now, don't you trouble yoreself, Miss Hester: me an' Freddie air a-goin' to git along all right. We ain't a-goin' to freeze, air we, Freddie, boy? Ah, not by a long sight; not ef Uncle 'Liph knows hisself."

All the time the genial man was talking, he was tucking the lap-robe snugly about the child and making him comfortable. Then he clucked to the old mare, and they rattled away.

There was a far-away look in Miss Prime's eyes as she watched them till they turned the corner and were out of sight. "I never did see sich a man as 'Liphalet Hodges. Why, a body'd think that he'd been married an' raised a whole houseful o' childern. He's worse 'n a old hen. An' it's marvellous the way Frederick took to him. Everybody calls the child Freddie. I must learn to call him that: it will make him feel more home-like, though it does sound foolish."

She went on with her work, but it was interrupted every now and then by strange fits of abstraction and revery, an unusual thing for this bustling and practical spinster. But then there are few of us but have had our hopes and dreams, and it would be unfair to think that Miss Hester was an exception. For once she had broken through her own discipline, and in her own kitchen was spending precious moments in dreams, and all because a man and a child had rattled away in a rickety buggy.

CHAPTER V

"**G**oodness gracious, Mis' Smith," exclaimed Mrs. Martin, rushing excitedly into the house of her next-door neighbour, "you'd ought to seen what I seen jest now."

"Do tell, Mis' Martin! What on airth was it?"

"Oh, I'm shore you'd never guess in the wide, wide world."

"An' I'm jest as shore that I ain't a-goin' to pester my head tryin' to: so go on an' tell me what it was."

"Lawsy me! what next'll happen, an' what does things mean, anyhow?"

"I can't tell you. Fur my part, I 'ain't heerd what 'things' air yit." Mrs. Smith was getting angry.

"My! Mis' Smith, don't git so impatient. Give me time to git my breath: it'll be enough, when I do tell you, to take away yore breath, jest like it did mine."

"Sallie Martin, you do beat all fur keepin' a body on the hooks."

"T ain't my fault, Mis' Smith. I declare I'm too astonished to speak. You know I was a-standin' in my window, not a-thinkin' nor expectin' nothin', jest like any person would, you know—"

"Yes, yes; go on."

"I was jest a-lookin' down the street, careless, when who should I see drive up to Miss Prime's door, an' hitch his hoss an' go in, but Brother 'Liphalet Hodges!"

"Well, sakes alive, Sallie Martin, I hope you ain't a-considerin' that strange. Why, you could 'a' seen that very same sight any time these fifteen years."

"But wait a minute till I tell you. I ain't done yit, by no means. The strange part 'ain't come. I thought I'd jest wait at the window and see how long Brother Hodges would stay: not that it was any o' my bus'ness, of course, or that I wanted to be a spyin' on anybody, but sorter fur—fur cur'osity, you know."

"Cert'n'y," said Mrs. Smith, feelingly. She could sympathise with such a sentiment.

"Well, after a while he come out a-smilin' as pleasant as a basket o' chips; an' I like to fell through the winder, fur he was a-leadin' by the hand—who do you suppose?"

"I 'ain't got a mortal idea who," said Mrs. Smith, "unless it was Miss Hester, an' they're married at last."

"No, indeed, 't wa'n't her. It was that little Brent boy that his mother died the other day."

"Sallie Martin, what air you a-tellin' me?"

"It's the gospel truth, Melviny Smith, as shore as I'm a-settin' here. Now what does it mean?"

"The good Lord only knows. Leadin' that little Brent boy? Ef it wasn't you a-settin' there tellin' me this, Mis' Martin, I wouldn't believe it. You don't suppose Hodges has took him to raise, do you?"

"How in the name of mercy is he goin' to raise any child, when there ain't no women folks about his house 'ceptin' old Marier, an' she so blind an' rheumaticky that she kin sca'cely git about?"

"Well, what's he a-doin' with the child, then?"

"That's jest what I'm a-goin' to find out. I'm a-goin' down to Miss Prime's. Len' me yore shawl, Melviny."

"You ain't never goin' to dare to ask her, air you?"

"You jest trust me to find things out without givin' myself away. I won't never let her know what I want right out, but I'll talk it out o' her."

"What a woman you air, Sallie Martin!" said Mrs. Smith, admiringly. "But do hurry back an' tell me what she says: I'm jest dyin' to know."

"I'll be back in little or no time, because I can't stay, nohow."

Mrs. Martin threw the borrowed shawl over her head and set off down the street. She and her friend were not dwellers on the mean street, and so they could pretend to so nearly an equal social footing with Miss Prime as to admit of an occasional neighbourly call.

Through the window Miss Prime saw her visitor approaching, and a grim smile curved the corners of her mouth. "Comin' fur news," muttered the spinster. "She'll git all she wants before she goes." But there was no trace of suspicion in her manner as she opened the door at Mrs. Martin's rap.

"Hey oh, Miss Hester, busy as usual, I see."

"Yes, indeed. People that try to do their dooty 'ain't got much time fur rest in this world."

"No, indeed; it's dig, dig, dig, and work, work, work."

"Take off yore shawl an' set down, Sallie. It's a wonder you don't take yore death o' cold or git plum full o' neuralgy, a-runnin' around in this weather with nothin' but a shawl over yore head."

"La, Miss Hester, they say that worthless people's hard to kill. It ain't allus true, though, fur there was poor Margar't Brent, she wasn't worth much, but my! she went out like a match."

"Yes, but matches don't go out until their time ef they're held down right; an' it's jest so with people."

"That's true enough, Miss Hester. Was you to Margar't's funeral?"

"Oh, yes, I went."

"Did you go out to the cimetery?"

"Oomph huh."

"Did she look natural?"

"Jest as natural as one could expect after a hard life an' a hard death."

"Pore Margar't!" Mrs. Martin sighed. There was a long and embarrassed silence. Miss Prime's lips were compressed, and she seemed more aggressively busy than usual. She bustled about as if every minute were her last one. She brushed off tables, set chairs to rights, and tried the golden-brown cup-cake with a straw to see if it were done. Her visitor positively writhed with curiosity and discomfiture. Finally she began again. "Margar't only had one child, didn't she?"

"Yes, that was all."

"Pore little lamb. Motherless childern has a hard time of it."

"Indeed, most of 'em do."

"Do you know what's become of the child, Miss Hester?"

"Yes, I do, Sallie Martin, an' you do too, or you wouldn't be a-settin' there beatin' about the bush, askin' me all these questions."

This sudden outburst gave Mrs. Martin quite a turn, but she exclaimed, "I declare to goodness, Miss Hester, I 'ain't heerd a livin' thing about it, only—"

She checked herself, but her relentless hostess caught at the word and demanded, "Only what, Mis' Martin?"

"Well, I seen Brother 'Liphalet Hodges takin' him away from here in his buggy—"

"An' so you come down to see what was what, eh, so's you could be the first to tell the neighbourhood?"

"Now, Miss Hester, you know that I ain't one o' them that talks, but I do feel sich an interest in the pore motherless child, an' when I seen Brother Hodges a-takin' him away, I thought perhaps he was a-goin' to take him to raise."

"Well, Brother Hodges ain't a-goin' to take him to raise."

"Mercy sakes! Miss Hester, don't git mad, but who is?"

"I am, that's who."

"Miss Prime, what air you a-sayin'? You shorely don't mean it. What kin you do with a child?"

"I kin train him up in the way he ought to go, an' keep him out o' other people's houses an' the street."

"Well, o' course, that's somethin'," said Mrs. Martin, weakly.

"Somethin'? Why, it's everything."

The visitor had now gotten the information for which she was looking, and was anxious to be gone. She was absolutely bursting with her news.

"Well, I must be goin'," she said, replacing her shawl and standing in embarrassed indecision. "I only run in fur a minute. I hope you 'ain't got no hard feelin's at my inquisitiveness."

"Not a bit of it. You wanted to know, an' you come and asked, that's all."

"I hope you'll git along all right with the child."

"I sha'n't stop at hopin'. I shall take the matter to the Lord in prayer."

"Yes, He knows best. Good-bye, Miss Hester."

"Good-bye, Sallie; come in ag'in." The invitation sounded a little bit sarcastic, and once more the grim smile played about Miss Prime's mouth.

"I 'low," she observed to herself, as she took the cake from the oven for the last time, tried it, and set it on the table,—"I 'low that I did give Sallie Martin one turn. I never did see sich a woman fur pryin' into other folks' business."

Swift are the wings of gossip, and swift were the feet of Mrs. Sallie Martin as she hurried back to tell the news to her impatient friend, who listened speechless with enjoyment and astonishment.

"Who would 'a' thought you could 'a' talked it out o' her so?" she gasped.

"Oh, I led her right along tell she told me everything," said Mrs. Martin, with a complacency which, remembering her reception, she was far from feeling.

Shortly after her departure, and while, no doubt, reinforced by Mrs. Smith, she was still watching at the window, 'Liphalet Hodges drove leisurely up to the door again.

"Well, Freddie," he said, as he helped the child to alight, "we've had a great time together, we have, an' we ain't frozen, neither: I told Miss Prime that she needn't be afeared. Don't drop yore jumpin'-jack, now, an' be keerful an' don't git yore hands on yore apron, 'cause they're kind o' sticky. Miss Hester 'u'd take our heads off ef we come back dirty."

The child's arms were full of toys,—a jumping-jack, a climbing monkey, a popgun, and the etceteras of childish amusement,—and his pockets and cheeks bulged with candy.

"La, 'Liphalet," exclaimed Miss Prime, when she saw them, "what on airth have you been a-buyin' that child—jumpin'-jacks an' sich things? They ain't a bit o' good, 'ceptin' to litter up a house an' put lightness in childern's minds. Freddie, what's that on yore apron? Goodness me! an' look at them hands—candy! 'Liphalet Hodges, I did give you credit fur better jedgment than this. Candy is the cause o' more aches an' pains than poison; an' some of it's reely coloured with ars'nic. How do you expect a child to grow up healthy an' with sound teeth when you feed him on candy?"

"Now, Miss Hester, now, now, now. I don't want to be a-interferin' with yore bus'ness; but it's jest like I said before, an' I will stick to it, you 'ain't never had no experunce in raisin' children. They can't git along jest on meat an' bread an' jam: they need candy—an'—ah—candy—an' sich things." Mr. Hodges ended lamely, looking rather guiltily at the boy's bulging pockets. "A little bit ain't a-goin' to hurt no child."

"'Liphalet, I've got a dooty to perform towards this motherless child, an' I ain't a-goin' to let no foolish notions keep me from performin' it."

"Miss Hester, I'm a-tryin' to follow Him that was a father to the fatherless an' a husband to the widow,—strange, that was made only to the widow,—an' I've got somethin' of a idee o' dooty myself. You may think I'm purty presumptuous, but I've took a notion into my head to kind o' help along a-raisin' Freddie. I ain't a-goin' to question yore authority, or nothin', but I thought mebbe you'd len' me the child once in a while to kind o' lighten up that old lonesome place o' mine: I know that Freddie won't object."

"Oh, 'Liphalet, do go 'long: I scarcely know whether you air a man or a child, sometimes."

"There's One that says, 'Except you become as a little child'—"

"'Liphalet, will you go 'long home?"

"I'spect I'd better be gittin' along.—Good-bye, Freddie; be a good boy, an' some day I'll take you up to my house an' let you ride old Bess around.—Good-bye, Miss Hester." And as he passed out to his buggy he whistled tenderly something that was whistled when he was a boy.

CHAPTER VI

The life of one boy is much like that of another. They all have their joys and their griefs, their triumphs and their failures, their loves and their hates, their friends and their foes, much as men have them in that maturer life of which the days of youth are an epitome. It would be rather an uninteresting task, and an entirely thankless one, to follow in detail the career of Frederick Brent as he grew from childhood to youth. But in order to understand certain traits that developed in his character, it will be necessary to note some, at least, of the circumstances that influenced his early life.

While Miss Prime grew to care for him in her own unemotional way, she had her own notions of how a boy should be trained, and those notions seemed to embody the repression of every natural impulse. She reasoned thus: "Human beings are by nature evil: evil must be crushed: ergo, everything natural must be crushed." In pursuance of this principle, she followed out a deliberate course of restriction, which, had it not been for the combating influence of Eliphalet Hodges, would have dwarfed the mental powers of the boy and cramped his soul beyond endurance. When he came of an age to play marbles, he was forbidden to play, because it was, to Miss Hester's mind, a species of gambling. Swimming was too dangerous to be for a moment considered. Fishing, without necessity, was wanton cruelty. Flying kites was foolishness and a waste of time.

The boy had shown an aptitude at his lessons that had created in his guardian's mind some ambition for him, and she held him down to his books with rigid assiduity. He was naturally studious, but the feeling that he was being driven made his tasks repellent, although he performed them without outward sign of rebellion, while he fumed within.

His greatest relaxations were his trips to and from his old friend Hodges. If Miss Prime crushed him, this gentle soul comforted him and smoothed out his ruffled feelings. It was this influence that kept him from despair. Away from his guardian, he was as if a chain that galled his flesh had been removed. And yet he could not hate Miss Hester, for it was constantly impressed upon him that all was being done for his good, and the word "duty" was burned like a fiery cross upon his heart and brain.

There is a bit of the pagan in every natural boy, and to give him too much to reverence taxes his powers until they are worn and impotent by the time he reaches manhood. Under Miss Hester's tutelage too many things became sacred to Fred Brent. It was wicked to cough in church, as it was a sacrilege to play with a hymn-book. His training was the apotheosis of the non-essential. But, after all, there is no rebel like Nature. She is an iconoclast.

When he was less than ten years old, an incident occurred that will in a measure indicate the manner of his treatment. Miss Prime's prescription for making a good boy was two parts punishment, two parts admonition, and six parts prayer. Accordingly, as the watchful and sympathetic neighbours said, "she an' that pore child fairly lived in church."

It was one class-meeting night, and, as usual, the boy and his guardian were sitting side by side at church. It was the habit of some of the congregation to bring their outside controversies into the class-room under the guise of testimonies or exhortations, and there to air their views where their opponents could not answer them. One such was Daniel Hastings. The trait had so developed in him that whenever he rose to speak, the question ran around, "I wonder who Dan'l's a-goin' to rake over the coals now." On this day he had been having a tilt with his old-time enemy, Thomas Donaldson, over the advent into Dexter of a young homœopathic doctor. With characteristic stubbornness, Dan'l had held that there was no good in any but the old-school medical men, and he sneered at the idea of anybody's being cured with sugar, as he contemptuously termed the pellets and powders affected by the new school. Thomas, who was considered something of a wit and who sustained his reputation by the perpetration of certain time-worn puns, had replied that other hogs were sugar-cured, and why not Dan'l? This had turned the laugh on Hastings, and he went home from the corner grocery, where the men were congregated, in high dudgeon.

Still smarting with the memory of his defeat, when he rose to speak that evening, he cast a glance full of unfriendly significance at his opponent and launched into a fiery exhortation on true religion.

"Some folks' religion," he said, "is like sugar, all sweetness and no power; but I want my religion like I want my medicine: I want it strong, an' I want it bitter, so's I'll know I've got it." In Fred Brent the sense of humour had not been entirely crushed, and the expression was too much for his gravity. He bowed his head and covered his mouth with his hand. He made no sound, but there were three pairs of eyes that saw the movement,—Miss Prime's, Eliphalet Hodges', and the Rev. Mr. Simpson's. Miss Prime's gaze was horrified, Mr. Simpson's stern; but in the eye of Mr. Hodges there was a most ungodly twinkle.

When Dan'l Hastings had finished his exhortation—which was in reality an arraignment of Thomas Donaldson's medical heresies—and sat down, the Rev. Mr. Simpson arose, and, bending an accusing glance upon the shrinking boy, began: "I perceive on the part of some of the younger members of the congregation a disposition towards levity. The house of God is not the place to find amusement. I never see young people deriding their elders without thinking of the awful lesson taught by the Lord's judgment upon those wicked youths whom the she-bears devoured. I never see a child laughing in church without trembling in spirit for his future. Some of the men whom I have seen in prison, condemned to death or a life of confinement, have begun their careers just in this way, showing disrespect for their elders and for the church. Beware, young people, who think you are smart and laugh and titter in the sanctuary; there is a prison waiting for you, there is a hell yawning for you. Behold, there is death in the pot!"

With a terrible look at the boy, Mr. Simpson sat down. There was much craning of necks and gazing about, but few in the church would have known to whom the pastor's remarks were addressed had not Miss Prime, at their conclusion, sighed in an injured way, and, rising with set lips, led the culprit out, as a criminal is led to the scaffold. How the boy suffered as, with flaming face, he walked down the aisle to the door, the cynosure of all eyes! He saw in the faces about him the accusation of having done a terrible thing, something unheard of and more wicked than he could understand. He felt revolted, child as he was, at the religion that made so much of his fault. Inwardly, he vowed that he would never "get religion" or go into a church when he was big enough to have his own way.

They had not gone far when a step approached them from behind, and Eliphalet Hodges joined them. Miss Prime turned tragically at his greeting, and broke out, "Don't reproach me 'Liphalet; it ain't no trainin' o' mine that's perduced a child that laughs at old foks in the Lord's house."

"I ain't a-goin' to reproach you, Miss Hester, never you fear; I ain't a-goin' to say a word ag'in' yore trainin'; but I jest thought I'd ask you not to be too hard on Freddie. You know that Dan'l is kind o' tryin' sometimes even to the gravity of older people; an' childern will be childern; they 'ain't got the sense, nor—nor—the deceit to keep a smooth face when they're a-laughin' all in their innards."

Miss Prime turned upon him in righteous wrath. "'Liphalet," she exclaimed, "I think it's enough fur this child to struggle ag'inst natural sin, without encouragin' him by makin' excuses fur him."

"It ain't my intention nor my desire to set a bad example before nobody, especially the young lambs of the flock, but I ain't a-goin' to blame Freddie fur doin' what many another of us wanted to do."

"'Deed an' double, that is fine talk fur you, 'Liphalet Hodges! you a trustee of the church, an' been a class-leader, a-holdin' up fur sich onregenerate carryin's-on."

"I ain't a-holdin' up fur nothin', Miss Hester, 'ceptin' nature an' the very couldn't-help-it-ness o' the thing altogether. I ain't a boy no more, by a good many years, but there's times when I've set under Dan'l Hastings's testimonies jest mortally cramped to laugh; an' ef it's so with a man, how will it be with a pore innercent child? I ain't a-excusin' natural sin in nobody. It wa'n't so much Freddie's natural sin as it was Dan'l's natural funniness." And there was something very like a chuckle in 'Liphalet's throat.

"'Liphalet, the devil's been puttin' fleas into yore ear, but I ain't a-goin' to let you argy me out o' none o' my settled convictions, although the Old Man's put plenty of argyment into yore head. That's his way o' capturin' a soul.—Walk on ahead, Frederick, an' don't be list'nin'. I'll 'tend to yore case later on."

"It's funny to me, Miss Hester, how it is that Christians know so much more about the devil's ways than they do about the Lord's. They're allus a-sayin', 'the Lord moves in a mysterious way,' but they kin allus put their finger on the devil."

"'Liphalet Hodges, that's a slur!"

"I ain't a-meanin' it as no slur, Miss Hester; but most Christians do seem to have a powerful fondness for the devil. I notice that they're allus admirin' his work an' praisin' up his sharpness, an' they'd be monstrous disappointed ef he didn't git as many souls as they expect."

"Well, after all the years that I've been a-workin' in the church an' a-tryin' to let my light so shine before the world, I didn't think that you'd be the one to throw out hints about my Christianity. But we all have our burdens to bear, an' I'm a-goin' to bear mine the best I kin, an' do my dooty, whatever comes of it." And Miss Hester gave another sigh of injured rectitude.

"I see, Miss Hester, that you're jest bent an' bound not to see what I mean, so I might as well go home."

"I think my mind ain't givin' way yit, an' I believe that I do understand plain words; but I ain't a-bearin' you no grudge. You've spoke yore mind, an' it's all right."

"But I hope there ain't no hard feelin's, after all these years."

"Oh, 'Liphalet, it ain't a part of even my pore weak religion to bear hard feelin's towards no one, no matter how they treat me. I'm jest tryin' to bear my cross an' suffer fur the Lord's sake."

"But I hope I ain't a-givin' you no cross to bear. I 'ain't never doubted yore goodness or yore Christianity: I only thought that mebbe yore methods, yore methods—"

Miss Prime's lips were drawn into a line. She divided that line to say, "I know what the Scriptures say: 'If thy right hand offend thee'"

"Hester, Hester!" he cried, stretching out his hands to her.

"Good-night, Brother Hodges. I must go in." She turned and left him standing at the gate with a hurt look in his face.

On going into the house, Miss Hester did not immediately 'tend to Fred, as she had promised. Instead, she left him and went into her own room where she remained awhile. When she came out, her lips were no less set, but her eyes were red. It is hardly to be supposed that she had been indulging in that solace of woman's woes, a good cry.

"Take off yore jacket, Freddie," she said, calmly, taking down a switch from over the clothes-press. "I'm a-goin' to whip you; but, remember, I ain't a-punishin' you because I'm mad. It's fur the purpose of instruction. It's fur yore own good."

Fred received his dressing-down without a whimper. He was too angry to cry. This Miss Prime took as a mark of especial depravity. In fact, the boy had been unable to discover any difference between an instructive and a vindictive whipping. It was perfectly clear in his guardian's mind, no doubt, but a cherry switch knows no such distinctions.

This incident only prepared Fred Brent for a further infraction of his guardian's rules the next day. One of Miss Prime's strictest orders had to do with fighting. Whatever the boys did to Fred, he was never to resent it. He must come to her, and she would go to the boy's mother. What an order to give a boy with muscles and fists and Nature strong within him! But, save for the telling, it had been obeyed, although it is hard to feel one's self an unwilling coward, a prig, and the laughingstock of one's fellows. But when, on the day after his unjust punishment, and while still stung by the sense of wrong, one of the petty schoolboy tyrants began to taunt him, he turned upon the young scamp and thrashed him soundly. His tormentor was not more hurt than surprised. Like most of his class, he was a tattler. The matter got to the teacher's ears, and that night Fred carried home an ominous-looking note. In his heart he believed that it meant another application of cherry switch, either instructive or vindictive, but he did not care. He had done the natural thing, and Nature rewards us for obeying her laws by making us happy or stoical. He had gone up in the estimation of his schoolfellows, even the thrashed one, and he felt a reckless joy. He would welcome a whipping. It would bring him back memories of what he had given Billy Tompkins. "Wouldn't Miss Hester be surprised," he thought, "if I should laugh out while she is whipping me?" And he laughed at the very thought. He was full of pleasure at himself. He had satisfied the impulse within him for once, and it made him happy.

Miss Prime read the ominous note, and looked at her charge thoughtfully. Fred glanced expectantly in the direction of the top of the clothes-press. But she only said, "Go out an' git in yore kindlin', Freddie; git yore chores done, an' then come in to supper." Her voice was menacingly quiet. The boy had learned to read the signs of her face too well to think that he was to get off so easily as this. Evidently, he would "get it" after supper, or Miss Prime had some new, refined mode of punishment in store for him. But what was it? He cudgelled his brain in vain, as he finished his chores, and at table he could hardly eat for wondering. But he might have spared himself his pains, for he learned all too soon.

Immediately after supper he was bidden to put on his cap and come along. Miss Prime took him by the hand. "I'm a-goin' to take you," she said, "to beg Willie Tompkins's pardon fur the way you did him."

Did the woman know what it meant to the boy? She could not,

or her heart would have turned against the cruelty. Fred was aghast. Beg his pardon! A whipping was a thousand times better: indeed, it would be a mercy. He began to protest, but was speedily silenced. The enforced silence, however, did not cool his anger. He had done what other boys did. He had acted in the only way that it seemed a boy could act under the circumstances, and he had expected to be punished as his fellows were; but this—this was awful. He clinched his hands until the nails dug into the palms. His face was as pale as death. He sweated with the consuming fire of impotent rage. He wished that he might run away somewhere where he could hide and tear things and swear. For a moment only he entertained the thought, and then a look into the determined face of the woman at his side drove the thought away. To his childish eyes, distorted by resentment, she was an implacable and relentless monster who would follow him with punishment anywhere he might go.

And now they were at Billy Tompkins's door. They had passed through, and he found himself saying mechanically the words which Miss Prime put into his mouth, while his tormentor grinned from beside his mother's chair. Then, after a few words between the women, in which he heard from Mrs. Tompkins the mysterious words, "Oh, I don't blame you, Miss Hester; I know that blood will tell," they passed out, and the grinning face of Billy Tompkins was the last thing that Fred saw. It followed him home. The hot tears fell from his eyes, but they did not quench the flames that were consuming him. There is nothing so terrible as the just anger of a child,—terrible in its very powerlessness. Polyphemus is a giant, though the mountain hold him down.

Next morning, when Fred went to school, Billy Tompkins with a crowd of boys about was waiting to deride him; but at sight of his face they stopped. He walked straight up to his enemy and began striking him with all his might.

"She made me beg your pardon, did she?" he gasped between the blows; "well, you take that for it, and that." The boys had fallen back, and Billy was attempting to defend himself.

"Mebbe she'll make me do it again to-night. If she does, I'll give you some more o' this to-morrow, and every time I have to beg your pardon. Do you hear?"

The boys cheered lustily, and Billy Tompkins, completely whipped and ashamed, slunk away.

That night no report of the fight went home. Fred Brent held the master hand.

In life it is sometimes God and sometimes the devil that comes to the aid of oppressed humanity. From the means, it is often hard to tell whose handiwork are the results.

CHAPTER VII

ynics and fools laugh at calf-love. Youth, which is wiser, treats it more seriously. When the boy begins to think of a girl, instead of girls, he displays the first budding signs of a real growing manhood. The first passion may be but the enthusiasm of discovery. Sometimes it is not. At times it dies, as fleeting enthusiasms do. Again it lives, and becomes a blessing, a curse, or a memory. Who shall say that the first half-sweet pang that strikes a boy's heart in the presence of the dear first girl is any less strong, intoxicating, and real to him than that which prompts him to take the full-grown woman to wife? With factitious sincerity we quote, "The boy is father to the man," and then refuse to believe that the qualities, emotions, and passions of the man are inherited from this same boy,—are just the growth, the development, of what was embryonic in him.

Nothing is more serious, more pleasant, and more diverting withal, than a boy's brooding or exultation—one is the complement of the other—over his first girl. As, to a great extent, a man is moulded by the woman he marries, so to no less a degree is a boy's character turned and shaped by the girl he adores. Either he descends to her level, or she draws him up, unconsciously, perhaps, to her own plane. Girls are missionaries who convert boys. Boys are mostly heathens. When a boy has a girl, he remembers to put on his cuffs and collars, and he doesn't put his necktie into his pocket on the way to school.

In a boy's life, the having of a girl is the setting up of an ideal. It is the new element, the higher something which abashes the unabashed, and makes John, who caused Henry's nose to bleed, tremble when little Mary stamps her foot. It is like an atheist's finding God, the sudden recognition of a higher and purer force against which all that he knows is powerless. Why doesn't John bully Mary? It would be infinitely easier than his former exploit with

37

Henry. But he does n't. He blushes in her presence, brings her the best apples, out of which heretofore he has enjoined the boys not to "take a hog-bite," and, even though the parental garden grow none, comes by flowers for her in some way, queer boyish bouquets where dandelions press shoulders with spring-beauties, daffodils, and roses,—strange democracy of flowerdom. He feels older and stronger.

In Fred's case the object of adoration was no less a person than Elizabeth Simpson, the minister's daughter. From early childhood they had seen and known each other at school, and between them had sprung up a warm childish friendship, apparently because their ways home lay along the same route. In such companionship the years sped; but Fred was a diffident boy, and he was seventeen and Elizabeth near the same before he began to feel those promptings which made him blushingly offer to carry her book for her as far as he went. She had hesitated, refused, and then assented, as is the manner of her sex and years. It had become a settled thing for them to walk home together, he bearing her burdens, and doing for her any other little service that occurred to his boyish sense of gallantry.

Without will of his own, and without returning the favour, he had grown in the Rev. Mr. Simpson's esteem. This was due mostly to his guardian's excellent work. In spite of his rebellion, training and environment had brought him greatly under her control, and when she began to admonish him about his lost condition spiritually she had been able to awaken a sort of superstitious anxiety in the boy's breast. When Miss Prime perceived that this had been accomplished, she went forthwith to her pastor and unburdened her heart.

"Brother Simpson," said she, "I feel that the Lord has appointed me an instrument in His hands for bringin' a soul into the kingdom." The minister put the tips of his fingers together and sighed piously and encouragingly. "I have been labourin' with Freddie in the sperrit of Christian industry, an' I believe that I have finally brought him to a realisin' sense of his sinfulness."

"H'm-m," said the minister. "Bless the Lord for this evidence of the activity of His people. Go on, sister."

"Freddie has at last come to the conclusion that hell is his lot unless he flees unto the mountain and seeks salvation."

"Bless the Lord for this."

"Now, Brother Simpson, I have done my part as fur as the Lord has showed me, except to ask you to come and wrastle with that boy."

"Let not thy heart be troubled, Sister Prime, for I will come as you ask me, and I will wrastle with that boy as Jacob did of old with the angel."

"Oh, Brother Simpson, I knowed you'd come. I know jest how you feel about pore wanderin' souls, an' I'm so glad to have yore strong arm and yore wisdom a-helpin' me."

"I hope, my sister, that the Lord may smile upon my poor labours, and permit us to snatch this boy as a brand from eternal burning."

"We shall have to labour in the sperrit, Brother Simpson."

"Yes, and with the understanding of the truth in our hearts and minds."

"I'm shore I feel mighty uplifted by comin' here to-day. Do come up to dinner Sunday, dear Brother Simpson, after preachin'."

"I will come, Sister Prime, I will come. I know by experience the worth of the table which the Lord provides for you, and then at the same season I may be able to sound this sinful boy as to his spiritual state and to drop some seed into the ground which the Lord has mercifully prepared for our harvest. Good-bye, sister, good-bye. I shall not forget, Sunday after preaching."

In accordance with his promise, the Rev. Mr. Simpson began to labour with Fred, with the result of driving him into a condition of dogged revolt, which only Miss Prime's persistence finally overcame. When revival time came round, as, sure as death it must come, Fred regularly went to the mourners' bench, mourned his few days until he had worked himself into the proper state, and then, somewhat too coldly, it is true, for his anxious guardian, "got religion."

On the visit next after this which Mr. Simpson paid to Miss Prime, he took occasion to say, "Ah, my sister, I am so glad that you pointed me to that lost lamb of the house of Israel, and I am thanking the Maker every day that He blessed my efforts to bring the straying one into the fold. Ah, there is more joy over the one lamb that is found than over the ninety and nine that went not astray!"

Mr. Simpson's parishioner acquiesced, but she had some doubts in her mind as to whose efforts the Lord had blessed. She felt a little bit selfish. She wanted to be the author of everything good that came to Fred. But she did not argue with Mr. Simpson. There are some concessions which one must make to one's pastor.

From this time on the preacher was Fred's friend, and plied him with good advice in the usual friendly way; but the boy bore it well, for Elizabeth smiled on him, and what boy would not bear a father's tongue for a girl's eyes?

The girl was like her mother, dark and slender and gentle. She had none of her father's bigness or bumptiousness. Her eyes were large and of a shade that was neither black nor brown. Her hair was very decidedly black. Her face was small, and round with the plumpness of youth, but one instinctively felt, in looking at it, that its lines might easily fall into thinness, even pitifulness, at the first touch of woman's sorrow. She was not, nor did she look to be, a strong girl. But her very weakness was the source of secret delight to the boy, for it made him feel her dependence on him. When they were together and some girlish fear made her cling to his arm, his heart swelled with pride and a something else that he could not understand and could not have described. Had any one told him that he was going through the half-sweet, half-painful, timid, but gallant first stages of love, he would have resented the imputation with blushes. His whole training would have made him think of such a thing with terror. He had learned never to speak of girls at home, for any reference to them by him was sure to bring forth from Miss Prime an instant and strong rebuke.

"Freddie," was the exclamation that gave his first unsuspecting remarks pause, "you're a-gittin' too fresh: you'd better be a-mindin' of yore studies, instead o' thinkin' about girls. Girls ain't a-goin' to make you pass yore examination, an', besides, you're a-gettin' mannish; fur boys o' yore age to be a-talkin' about girls is mannish, do you hear, sir? You're a-beginnin' to feel yore keepin' too strong. Don't let me hear no more sich talk out o' you."

There never was a manly boy in the world whom the word "mannish," when applied to him, did not crush. It is a horrid word, nasty and full of ugly import. Fred was subdued by it, and so kept silence about his female friends. Happy is the boy who dares at home to pour out his heart about the girls he knows and likes, and thrice unhappy he who through mistaken zeal on the part of misguided parents is compelled to keep his thoughts in his heart and brood upon his little aproned companions as upon a secret sin. Two things are thereby engendered, stealth and unhealth. If Fred escaped certain youthful pitfalls, it was because he was so repressed that he had learned to hide himself from himself, his thoughts from the mind that produced them.

He was a boy strong and full of blood. The very discipline that had given a gloomy cast to his mind had given strength and fortitude to his body. He was austere, because austerity was all that he had ever known or had a chance of knowing; but too often austerity is but the dam that holds back the flood of potential passion. Not to know the power which rages behind the barricade is to leave the structure weak for a hapless day when, carrying all before it, the flood shall break its bonds and in its fury ruin fair field and smiling mead. It was well for Fred Brent that the awakening came when it did.

In the first days of June, when examinations are over, the annual exhibition done, and the graduating class has marched away proud in the possession of its diplomas, the minds of all concerned turn naturally towards the old institution, the school picnic. On this occasion parents join the teachers and pupils for a summer day's outing in the woods. Great are the preparations for the festal day, and great the rejoicings thereon. For these few brief hours old men and women lay aside their cares and their dignity and become boys and girls again. Those who have known sorrow—and who has not?—take to themselves a day of forgetfulness. Great baskets are loaded to overflowing with the viands dear to the picnicker's palate,—sandwiches whose corpulence would make their sickly brothers of the railway restaurant wither with envy, pies and pickles, cheese and crackers, cakes and jams galore. Old horses that, save for this day, know only the market-cart or the Sunday chaise, are hitched up to bear out the merry loads. Old waggons, whose wheels have known no other decoration than the mud and clay of rutty roads, are festooned gaily with cedar wreaths, oak leaves, or the gaudy tissue-paper rosettes, and creak joyfully on their mission of lightness and mirth. On foot, by horse, in waggon or cart, the crowds seek some neighbouring grove, and there the day is given over to laughter, mirth, and song. The children roll and tumble on the sward in the intoxication of "swing-turn" and "ring-around-a-rosy." The young women, with many blushes and shy glances, steal off to quiet nooks with their imploring swains. Some of the elders, anxious to prove that they have not yet lost all their youth and agility, indulge, rather awkwardly perhaps, in the exhausting amusement of the jumping-rope. A few of the more staid walk apart in conversation with some favourite pastor who does not decline to take part in the innocent pleasures and crack ponderous jokes for the edification of his followers. Perhaps some of the more daring are engaged in one of the numerous singing plays, such as "Oh, la, Miss Brown," or "Swing Candy, Two and Two," but these are generally frowned upon: they are too much like dancing, and time has been when some too adventurous church-member has been "churched" for engaging in one.

In such a merrymaking was the community which surrounded the high school at Dexter engaged when the incident occurred which opened Fred's eyes to his own state. Both he and Elizabeth had been in the prize ranks that year, and their friends had turned out in full and made much of them. Even Eliphalet Hodges was there, with old Bess festooned as gaily as the other horses, and both Miss Prime and Mr. Simpson were in evidence. The afternoon of the day was somewhat advanced, the dinner had been long over, and the weariness of the people had cast something of a quietus over the hilarity of their sports. They were sitting about in groups, chatting and laughing, while the tireless children were scurrying about in games of "tag," "catcher," and "hide-and-seek."

The grove where the festivities were being held was on a hillside which sloped gently to the bank of a small, narrow stream, usually dry in summer; but now, still feeling the force of the spring freshets, and swollen by the rain of the day before, it was rushing along at a rapid rate. A fence divided the picnic-ground proper from the sharper slope of the rivulet's bank. This fence the young people had been warned not to pass, and so no danger was apprehended on account of the stream's overflowing condition. But the youngsters at Dexter were no more obedient than others of their age elsewhere. So when a scream arose from several childish voices at the lower part of the hill, everybody knew that some child had been disobeying, and, pell-mell, the picnickers rushed in the direction of the branch.

When they reached the nearest point from which they could see the stream, a terrifying sight met their eyes. A girl was struggling in the shallow but swift water. She had evidently stepped on the sloping bank and fallen in. Her young companions were running alongside the rivulet, stretching out their hands helplessly to her, but the current was too strong, and, try as she would, she could not keep her feet. A cry of grief and despair went up from the girls on the bank, as she made one final effort and then fell and was carried down by the current.

Men were leaping the fence now, but a boy who had seen the

whole thing from a neighbouring hillock was before them. Fred Brent came leaping down the hill like a young gazelle. He had seen who the unfortunate girl was,—Elizabeth,—and he had but one desire in his heart, to save her. He reached the bank twenty yards ahead of any one else, and plunged into the water just in front of her, for she was catching and slipping, clinging and losing hold, but floating surely to her death. He struggled up stream, reached and caught her by the dress. The water tugged at him and tried to throw him over, but he stemmed it, and, lifting her up in his arms, fought his way manfully to the bank. Up this he faltered, slipping and sliding in the wet clay, and weak with his struggle against the strong current. But his face was burning and his blood tingling as he held the girl close to him till he gave her unconscious form into her father's arms.

For the moment all was confusion, as was natural when a preacher's daughter was so nearly drowned. The crowd clustered around and gave much advice and some restoratives. Some unregenerate, with many apologies and explanations concerning his possession, produced a flask, and part of the whisky was forced down the girl's throat, while her hands and face and feet were chafed. She opened her eyes at last, and a fervent "Thank God!" burst from her father's lips and called forth a shower of Amens.

"I allus carry a little somethin' along, in case of emergencies," explained the owner of the flask as he returned it to his pocket, with a not altogether happy look at its depleted contents.

As soon as Fred saw that Elizabeth was safe, he struck away for home, unobserved, and without waiting to hear what the crowd were saying. He heard people calling his name kindly and admiringly, but it only gave wings to the feet that took him away from them. If he had thrown the girl in instead of bringing her out, he could not have fled more swiftly or determinedly away from the eyes of people. Tired and footsore, drenched to the skin and chilled through, he finally reached home. He was trembling, he was crying, but he did not know it, and had he known, he could not have told why. He did not change his clothes, but crouched down in a corner and hid his face in his hands. He dreaded seeing any one or hearing any person speak his name. He felt painfully conscious of a new self, which he thought must be apparent to other eyes.

The accident of the afternoon had cast a gloom over the merry-makings, and, the picnic breaking up abruptly, sent the people scurrying home, so that Miss Prime was at the house not far behind her charge.

"Freddie," she called to him as she entered the house, "Freddie, where air you?" And then she found him. She led him out of the corner and looked him over with a scrutinising eye. "Freddie Brent," she said solemnly, "you've jest ruined yore suit." He was glad. He wanted to be scolded. "But," she went on, "I don't care ef you have." And here she broke down. "You're a-goin' to have another one, fur you're a right smart boy, that's all I've got to say." For a moment he wanted to lay his head on her breast and give vent to the sob which was choking him. But he had been taught neither tenderness nor confidence, so he choked back the sob, though his throat felt dry and hot and strained. He stood silent and embarrassed until Miss Prime recovered herself and continued: "But la, child, you'll take yore death o' cold. Git out o' them wet things an' git into bed, while I make you some hot tea. Fur the life o' me, I never did see sich carryin's-on."

The boy was not sorry to obey. He was glad to be alone. He drank the warm tea and tried to go to sleep, but he could not. His mind was on fire. His heart seemed as if it would burst from his bosom. Something new had come to him. He began to understand, and blushed because he did understand. It was less discovery than revelation. His forehead was hot. His temples were throbbing. It was well that Miss Prime did not discover it: she would have given him horehound to cure—thought!

From the moment that the boy held the form of the girl to his heart he was changed, and she was changed to him. They could never be the same to each other again. Manhood had come to him in a single instant, and he saw in her womanhood. He began for the first time to really know himself, and it frightened him and made him ashamed.

He drew the covers over his head and lay awake, startled, surprised at what he knew himself and mankind to be.

To Fred Brent the awakening had come,—early, if we would be prudish; not too early, if we would be truthful.

CHAPTER VIII

I f Fred Brent had needed anything to increase his consciousness of the new feeling that had come to him, he could not have done better to get it than by going to see Eliphalet Hodges next day. His war of thought had gone on all night, and when he rose in the morning he thought that he looked guilty, and he was afraid that Miss Prime would notice it and read his secret. He wanted rest. He wanted to be secure from any one who would even suspect what was in his heart. But he wanted to see and to talk to some one. Who better, then, than his old friend?

So he finished his morning's chores and slipped away. He would not pass by Elizabeth's house, but went by alleys and lanes until he reached his destination. The house looked rather silent and deserted, and Mr. Hodges' old assistant did not seem to be working in the garden as usual. But after some search the boy found his old friend smoking upon the back porch. There was a cloud upon the usually bright features, and the old man took his pipe from his mouth with a disconsolate sigh as the boy came in sight.

"I'm mighty glad you've come, Freddie," said he, in a sad voice. "I've been a-wantin' to talk to you all the mornin'. Set down on the side o' the porch, or git a chair out o' the house, ef you'd ruther."

The boy sat down, wondering what could be the matter with his friend, and what he could have to say to him. Surely it must be something serious, for the whole tone and manner of his companion indicated something of import. The next remark startled him into sudden suspicion.

"There's lots o' things made me think o' lots of other things in the last couple o' days. You've grown up kind o' quick like, Freddie, so that a body 'ain't hardly noticed it, but that ain't no matter. You're up or purty nigh it, an' you can understand and appreciate lots o' the things that you used to couldn't."

Fred sat still, with mystery and embarrassment written on his

45

face. He wanted to hear more, but he was almost afraid to listen further.

"I 'ain't watched you so close, mebbe, as I'd ought to 'a' done, but when I seen you yistiddy evenin' holdin' that little girl in yore arms I said to myself, I said, "Liphalet Hodges, Freddie ain't a child no more; he's growed up.'" The boy's face was scarlet. Now he was sure that the thoughts of his heart had been surprised, and that this best of friends thought of him as "fresh," "mannish," or even wicked. He could not bear the thought of it; again the tears rose in his eyes, usually so free from such evidences of weakness. But the old man went on slowly in a low, half-reminiscent tone, without looking at his auditor to see what effect his words had had. "Well, that was one of the things that set me thinkin'; an' then there was another." He cleared his throat and pulled hard at his pipe; something made him blink,—dust, or smoke, or tears, perhaps. "Freddie," he half sobbed out, "old Bess is dead. Pore old Bess died last night o' colic. I'm afeared the drive to the picnic was too much fur her."

"Old Bess dead!" cried the boy, grieved and at the same time relieved. "Who would have thought it? Poor old girl! It seems like losing one of the family."

"She was one of the family," said the old man brokenly. "She was more faithful than most human beings." The two stood sadly musing, the boy as sad as the man. "Old Bess" was the horse that had taken him for his first ride, that winter morning years before, when the heart of the child was as cold as the day. Eliphalet Hodges had warmed the little heart, and, in the years that followed, man, child, and horse had grown nearer to each other in a queer but sympathetic companionship.

Then, as if recalling his mind from painful reflections, the elder man spoke again. "But it ain't no use a-worryin' over what can't be helped. We was both fond o' old Bess, an' I know you feel as bad about losin' her as I do. But I'm a-goin' to give her a decent burial, sich as a Christian ought to have; fur, while the old mare wasn't no perfessor, she lived the life, an' that's more 'n most perfessors do. Yes, sir, I'm a-goin' to have her buried: no glue-man fur me. I reckon you're a-wantin' to know how old Bess dyin' an' yore a-savin' 'Lizabeth could run into each other in my mind; but they did. Fur, as I see you standin' there a-holdin' the little girl, it come to me sudden like, 'Freddie's grown now, an' he'll be havin' a girl of his own purty soon, ef he 'ain't got one now. Mebbe it'll be 'Lizabeth.'" The old man paused for a moment; his eyes rested on the boy's fiery face. "Tut, tut," he resumed, "you ain't ashamed, air you? Well, what air you a-gittin' so red fur? Havin' a girl ain't nothin' to be ashamed of, or skeered about neither. Most people have girls one time or another, an' I don't know of nothin' that'll make a boy or a young man go straighter than to know that his girl's eyes air upon him. Don't be ashamed at all."

Fred still blushed, but he felt better, and his face lightened over the kindly words.

"I didn't finish tellin' you, though, what I started on. I got to thinkin' yesterday about my young days, when I had a girl, an' how I used to ride back an' forth on the pore old horse right into this town to see her; an' as I drove home from the picnic I talked to the old nag about it, an' she whisked her tail an' laid back her ears, jest like she remembered it all. It was on old Bess that I rode away from my girl's house after her first 'no' to me, an' it seemed then that the animal sympathised with me, fur she drooped along an' held down her head jest like I was a-doin'. Many a time after that we rode off that way together, fur the girl was set in her ways, an' though she confessed to a hankerin' fur me, she wanted to be independent. I think her father put the idee into her head, fur he was a hard man, an' she was his all, his wife bein' dead. After a while we stopped talkin' about the matter, an' I jest went an' come as a friend. I only popped the question once more, an' that was when her father died an' she was left all alone.

"It was a summer day, warm an' cheerful like this, only it was evenin', an' we was a-settin' out on her front garden walk. She was a-knittin', an' I was a-whippin' the groun' with a switch that I had brought along to touch Bess up with now an' then. I had hitched her out front, an' she kep' a-turnin' her eyes over the fence as ef she was as anxious as I was, an' that was mighty anxious. Fin'ly I got the question out, an' the girl went all red in a minute: she had been jest a purty pink before. Her knittin' fell in her lap. Fust she started to answer, then she stopped an' her eyes filled up. I seen she was a-weak'nin', so I thought I'd push the matter. 'Come,' says I, gentle like, an' edgin' near up to her, 'give me my answer. I been waitin' a long time fur a yes.' With that she grabbed knittin', apron, an' all, an' put 'em to her eyes an' rushed into the house. I knowed she'd gone in to have a good cry an' settle her nerves, fur that's the way all women-folks does: so I knowed it was no use to bother her until it was done.

So I walks out to the fence, an', throwin' an arm over old Bess's back, I told her all about it, jest as I'm a-tellin' you, she a-lookin' at me with her big meltin' eyes an' whinnyin' soft like.

"After a little while the girl come out. She was herself ag'in, but there was a look in her face that turned my heart stone-cold. Her voice sounded kind o' sharp as she said, "Liphalet, I've been a-thinkin' over what you said. I'm only a woman, an' I come purty near bein' a weak one; but I'm all right now. I don't mind tellin' you that ef I was ever goin' to marry, you'd be my choice, but I ain't a-goin' to have my father's sperrit a-thinkin' that I took advantage of his death to marry you. Good-bye, 'Liphalet.' She held out her hand to me, an' I took it. 'Come an' see me sometimes,' she said. I couldn't answer, so I went out and got on old Bess an' we jogged away. It was an awful disappointment, but I thought I would wait an' let my girl come aroun', fur sometimes they do,—in fact mostly; but she has never give me a sign to make me think that she has. That was twenty years ago, an' I've been waitin' faithful ever sence. But it seems like she was different from most women, an''specially good on holdin' out. People that was babies then have growed up an' married. An' now the old companion that has been with me through all this waitin' has left me. I know what it means. It means that I'm old, that years have been wasted, that chances have been lost. But you have taught me my lesson, Bess. Dear old Bess, even in yore last hours you did me a service, an' you, Freddie, you have given me the stren'th that I had twenty years ago, an' I'm a-goin' to try to save what remains of my life. I never felt how alone I was until now." He was greatly agitated. He rose and grasped the boy's arm. "Come, Freddie," he said; "come on. I'm a-goin' ag'in to ask Miss Prime to be my wife."

"Miss Prime!" exclaimed Fred, aghast.

"Miss Prime was my sweetheart, Freddie, thirty years ago, jest like 'Lizabeth is yor'n now. Come along."

The two set out, Hodges stepping with impatient alacrity, and the boy too astounded to speak.

It was a beautiful morning at the end of June. The sense of spring's reviving influence had not yet given way to the full languor and sensuousness of summer. The wind was soft and warm and fragrant. The air was full of the song of birds and the low droning of early bees. The river that flowed between the green hills and down through Dexter was like a pane of wrinkled glass, letting light and joy even into the regions below. Over the streets and meadows and hills lay a half haze, like a veil over the too dazzling beauty of an Eastern princess. The hum of business—for in the passing years Dexter had grown busy—the roar of traffic in the streets, all melted into a confused and intoxicating murmur as the pedestrians passed into the residence portion of the town to the cottage where Miss Prime still lived. The garden was as prim as ever, the walks as straight and well kept. The inevitable white curtains were fluttering freshly from the window, over which a huge matrimony vine drooped lazily and rung its pink and white bells to invite the passing bees.

Eliphalet paused at the gate and heaved a deep sigh. So much depended upon the issue of his present visit. The stream of his life had been flowing so smoothly before. Now if its tranquillity were disturbed it never could be stilled again. Did he dare to risk so much upon so hazardous a chance? Were it not better to go back home, back to his old habits and his old ease, without knowing his fate? That would at least leave him the pleasure of speculating. He might delude himself with the hope that some day—He faltered. His hand was on the gate, but his face was turned back towards the way he had come. Should he enter, or should he go back? Fate decided for him, for at this juncture the door opened, and Miss Hester appeared in the doorway and called out, "Do come in, 'Liphalet. What air you a-standin' out there so long a-studyin' about, fur all the world like a bashful boy?"

The shot told. He was a bashful boy again, going fearfully, tremblingly, lovingly, to see the girl of his heart; but there was no old Bess to whinny encouragement to him from over the little fence. If he blushed, even the scrutinising eyes of Miss Prime did not see it, for the bronze laid on his face by summers and winters of exposure; but he felt the hot blood rush up to his face and neck, and the perspiration breaking out on his brow. He paused long enough to mop his face, and then, saying to Fred, in a low tone, "You stay in the garden, my boy, until it's all over," he opened the gate and entered in the manner of one who leads a forlorn hope through forest aisles where an ambush is suspected. The door closed behind him. Interested, excited, wondering and fearing, doubting and hoping, Fred remained in the garden. There were but two thoughts in his head, and they were so new and large that his poor boy's cranium had room for no more. They ran in this wise: "Miss Prime is Uncle 'Liphalet's girl, and Elizabeth is mine."

Within, Miss Prime was talking on in her usual decided fashion, while the man sat upon the edge of his chair and wondered how he could break in upon the stream of her talk and say what was in his heart. At last the lady exclaimed, "I do declare, 'Liphalet, what kin be the matter with you? You 'ain't said ten words sence you've been a-settin' there. I hope you 'ain't talked yoreself entirely out with Fred. It does beat all how you an' that boy seem to grow thicker an' thicker every day. One 'ud think fur all the world that you told him all yore secrets, an' was afeared he'd tell 'em, by the way you stick by him; an' he's jest as bad about you. It's amazin'."

"Freddie's a wonderful good boy, an' he's smart, too. They ain't none of 'em a-goin' to throw dust in his eyes in the race of life."

"I'm shore I've tried to do my dooty by him the very best I could, an' ef he does amount to anything in this world it'll be through hard labour an' mighty careful watchin'." Miss Hester gave a sigh that was meant to be full of solemnity, but that positively reeked with self-satisfaction.

"But as you say, 'Liphalet," she went on, "Fred ain't the worst boy in the world, nor the dumbest neither, ef I do say it myself. I ain't a-sayin', mind you, that he's anything so great or wonderful; but I've got to thinkin' that there's somethin' in him besides original sin, an' I should feel that the Lord had been mighty favourin' to me ef I could manage to draw it out. The fact of it is, 'Liphalet, I've took a notion in my head about Fred, an' I'm a-goin' to tell you what it is. I've decided to make a preacher out o' him."

"H'm—ah—well, Miss Hester, don't you think you'd better let the Lord do that?"

"Nonsense, 'Liphalet! you 'ain't got no insight at all. I believe in people a-doin' their part an' not a-shovin' everything off on the Lord. The shiftless don't want nothin' better than to say that they will leave the Lord to take care o' things, an' then fold their arms an' set down an' let things go to the devil. Remember, Brother Hodges, I don't mean that in a perfane way. But then, because God made the sunlight an' the rain, it ain't no sign that we shouldn't prune the vine."

Miss Hester's face had flushed up with the animation of her talk, and her eyes were sparkling with excitement.

Eliphalet looked at her, and his heart leaped. He felt that the time had come to speak.

"Miss Hester," he began, and the hat in his hand went round and round nervously.

50

"'Liphalet, fur goodness' sake do lay yore hat on the table. You'll ruin the band of it, an' you make me as nervous as a cat."

He felt a little dampened after this, but he laid down the offending hat and began again. "I've been thinkin' some myself, Miss Hester, an' it's been about you."

"About me? La, 'Liphalet, what have you been a-thinkin' now?" The "now" sounded as if his thoughts were usually rather irresponsible.

"It was about you an'—an'—old Bess."

"About me an' old Bess! Bless my soul, man, will you stop beatin' about the bush an' tell me what on airth I've got to do with yore horse?"

"Old Bess is dead, Miss Hester; died last night o' colic."

"Well, I thought there was somethin' the matter with you. I'm mighty sorry to hear about the poor old creatur; but she'd served you a long while."

"That's jest what set me a-thinkin': she has served me a long while, an' now she's dead. Do you know what that means, Miss Hester? It means that we're a-gittin' old, you an' me. Do you know when I got old Bess? It was nigh thirty years ago: I used to ride her up to this door an' tie her to that tree out there: it was a saplin' then. An' now she's dead."

The man's voice trembled, and his listener was strangely silent.

"You know on what errands the old horse used to bring me," he went on, "but it wasn't to be,—then. Hester," he rose, went over to her, and looked down into her half-averted face, which went red and pale by turns,—"Hester, 'ain't we wasted time enough?"

There was a long pause before she lifted her face: he stood watching her with the light of a great eagerness in his eyes. At last she spoke. There was a catch in her voice; it was softer than usual.

"'Liphalet," she began, "I'm right glad you remember those days. I 'ain't never furgot 'em myself. It's true you've been a good, loyal friend to me, an' I thank you fur it, but, after all these years—"

He broke in upon her with something like youthful impetuosity. "After all these years," he exclaimed, "an endurin' love ought to be rewarded. Hester, I ain't a-goin' to take 'no' fur an answer. I've got lots o' years o' life in me yet,—we both have,—an' I ain't a-goin' on with an empty home an' an empty heart no longer."

"'Liphalet, you ain't a young man no more, an' I ain't a young woman, an' the Lord—"

"I don't care ef I ain't; an' I don't believe in shovin' everything off on the Lord."

"'Liphalet!" It was a reproach.

"Hester!" This was love. He put his arm around her and kissed her. "You're a-goin' to say yes, ain't you? You ain't a-goin' to send me away miserable? You're a-dyin' to say yes, but you're a-tryin' to force yoreself not to. Don't." He lifted her face as a young lover might, and looked down into her eyes. "Is it yes?"

"Well, 'Liphalet it 'pears like you're jest so pesterin' that I've got to say yes. Yes, then." And she returned the quiet but jubilant kiss that he laid upon her lips.

"After all these years," he said. "Sorrow may last fur a night, but joy cometh in the mornin'. It was a long night, but, thank the Lord, mornin''s broke." Then, rising, he went to the door and called joyously, "Freddie, come on in: it's all over."

"'Liphalet, did that boy know what you was a-goin' to say?"

"Yes, o' course he did."

"Oh, my! oh, my! Well, I've got a good mind to take it all back. Oh, my!" And when Fred came in, for the first time in her life Miss Prime was abashed and confused in his presence.

But Eliphalet had no thought of shame. He took her by the hand and said, "Freddie, Miss Hester's consented at last: after thirty years, she's a-goin' to marry me."

But Miss Hester broke in, "'Liphalet, don't be a-puttin' notions in that boy's head. You go 'way, Fred, right away."

Fred went out, but he felt bolder. He went past Elizabeth's house whistling. He didn't care. He wondered if he would have to wait thirty years for her. He hoped not.

CHAPTER IX

So great has been our absorption in the careers of Fred Brent, Miss Prime, and Eliphalet Hodges that we have sadly neglected some of the characters whose acquaintance we made at the beginning of our story. But nature and Time have been kinder,—or more cruel, if you will. They have neither passed over nor neglected them. They have combined with trouble and hard work to kill one of Fred's earliest friends. Melissa Davis is no more, and the oldest girl, Sophy, supplements her day's work of saleswoman in a dry-goods store by getting supper in the evening and making the younger Davises step around. Mrs. Warren, the sometime friend of Margaret Brent and enemy of Miss Prime, has moved farther out, into the suburbs, for Dexter has suburbs now, and boasts electric cars and amusement parks. Time has done much for the town. Its streets are paved, and the mean street that bore the tumble-down Brent cottage and its fellows has been built up and grown respectable. It and the street where Miss Prime's cottage frowned down have settled away into a quiet residential portion of the town, while around to the east, south, and west, and on both sides of the little river that divides the city, roars and surges the traffic of a characteristic middle-West town. Half-way up the hill, where the few aristocrats of the place formerly lived in almost royal luxuriance and seclusion, a busy sewing-machine factory has forced its way, and with its numerous chimneys and stacks literally smoked the occupants out; at their very gates it sits like the commander of a besieging army, and about it cluster the cottages of the workmen, in military regularity. Little and neat and trim, they flock there like the commander's obedient host, and such they are, for the sight of them offends the eyes of wealth. So, what with the smoke, and what with the proximity of the poorer classes, wealth capitulates, evacuates, and, with robes discreetly held aside, passes by to another quarter, and a new district is born where poverty dare not penetrate. Seated on a hill, where, as is their inclination, they may look down, literally and figuratively, upon the hurrying town, they are complacent again, and the new-comers to the town, the new-rich magnates and the half-rich strugglers who would be counted on the higher level, move up and swell their numbers at Dexter View.

Amid all this change, two alone of those we know remain unaltered and unalterable, true to their traditions. Mrs. Smith and Mrs. Martin, the two ancient gossips, still live side by side, spying and commenting on all that falls within their ken, much as they did on that day when 'Liphalet Hodges took Fred Brent for his first drive behind old Bess. Their windows still open out in the same old way, whence they can watch the happenings of the street. If there has been any change in them at all, it is that they have grown more absorbed and more keen in following and dissecting their neighbours' affairs.

It is to these two worthies, then, that we wish to reintroduce the reader on an early autumn evening some three months after the events narrated in the last chapter.

Mrs. Martin went to her back fence, which was the nearest point of communication between her and her neighbour. "Mis' Smith," she called, and her confederate came hurrying to the door, thimble on and a bit of sewing clutched precariously in her apron, just as she had caught it up when the significant call brought her to the back door.

"Oh, you're busy as usual, I see," said Mrs. Martin.

"It ain't nothin' partic'ler, only a bit o' bastin' that I was doin'."

"You ain't a-workin' on the machine, then, so you might bring your sewin' over and take a cup o' tea with me."

"La! now that's so kind o' you, Mis' Martin. I was jest thinkin' how good a cup o' tea would taste, but I didn't want to stop to make it. I'll be over in a minute, jest as soon as I see if my front door is locked." And she disappeared within the house, while Mrs. Martin returned to her own sitting-room.

The invited knew very well what the invitation to tea meant. She knew that some fresh piece of news was to be related and discussed. The beverage of which she was invited to partake was but a pretext, but neither the one nor the other admitted as much. Each understood perfectly, as by a tacit agreement, and each tried to deceive herself and the other as to motives and objects.

There is some subtle tie between tea-drinking and gossip. It is over their dainty cups that women dissect us men and damn their sisters. Some of the quality of the lemon they take in their tea gets into their tongues. Tea is to talk what dew is to a plant, a gentle nourishing influence, which gives to its product much of its own quality. There are two acids in the tea which cultured women take. There is only one in the beverage brewed by commonplace people. But that is enough.

Mrs. Martin had taken her tray into the sitting-room, where a slight fire was burning in the prim "parlour cook," on which the hot water was striving to keep its quality when Mrs. Smith came in.

"La, Mis' Martin, you do manage to have everything so cosy. I'm shore a little fire in a settin'-room don't feel bad these days."

"I jest thought I'd have to have a fire," replied Mrs. Martin, "fur I was feelin' right down chilly, though goodness knows a person does burn enough coal in winter, without throwin' it away in these early fall days."

"Well, the Lord's put it here fur our comfort, an' I think we're a-doin' His will when we make use o' the good things He gives us."

"Ah, but Mis' Smith, there's too many people that goes about the world thinkin' that they know jest what the Lord's will is; but I have my doubts about 'em, though, mind you, I ain't a-mentionin' no names: 'no name, no blame.'" Mrs. Martin pressed her lips and shook her head, a combination of gestures that was eloquent with meaning. It was too much for her companion. Her curiosity got the better of her caution.

"Dear me!" she exclaimed. "What is it now?"

"Oh, nothin' of any consequence at all. It ain't fur me to be a-judgin' my neighbours or a-talkin' about 'em. I jest thought I'd have you over to tea, you're sich good company."

Mrs. Smith was so impatient that she had forgotten her sewing and it lay neglected in her lap, but in no other way did she again betray her anxiety. She knew that there was something new to be told and that it would be told all in good time. But when gossip has become a fine art it must be conducted with dignity and precision.

"Let me see, I believe you take two lumps o' sugar an' no milk." Mrs. Martin knew perfectly what her friend took. "I don't know how this tea is. I got it from the new grocery over at the corner." She tasted it deliberately. "It might 'a' drawed a little more." Slowly she stirred it round and round, and then, as if she had drawn the truth from the depths of her cup, she observed, "This is a queer world, Mis' Smith."

Mrs. Smith sighed a sigh that was appreciative and questioning at once. "It is indeed," she echoed; "I'm always a-sayin' to myself what a mighty cur'us world this is."

"Have you ever got any tea from that new grocery-man?" asked her companion, with tantalising irrelevance.

"No: I hain't never even been in there."

"Well, this here's middlin' good; don't you think so?"

"Oh, it's more than middlin', it's downright good. I think I must go into that grocery some time, myself."

"I was in there to-day, and met Mis' Murphy: she says there's great goin'-ons up at Miss Prime's—I never shall be able to call her Mis' Hodges."

"You don't tell me! She and Brother 'Liphalet 'ain't had a fallin' out already, have they? Though what more could you expect?"

"Oh, no, indeed. It ain't no fallin' out, nothin' o' the kind."

"Well, what then? What has Miss Hester—I mean Mis' Hodges been doin' now? Where will that woman stop? What's she done?"

"Well, you see,—do have another cup of tea, an' help yoreself to that bread an' butter,—you see, Freddie Brent has finished at the high school, an' they've been wonderin' what to make him."

"Well, what air they a-goin' to make him? His father was a good stone-mason, when he was anything."

"Humph! you don't suppose Miss Hester's been sendin' a boy to school to learn Latin and Greek an' algebry an' sich, to be a stone-mason, do you? Huh uh! Said I to myself, as soon as I see her sendin' him from the common school to high school, says I, 'she's got big notions in her head.' Oh, no; the father's trade was not good enough fur her boy: so thinks Mis' 'Liphalet Hodges."

"Well, what on airth is she goin' to make out of him, then?"

"Please pass me that sugar: thank you. You know Mr. Daniels offered him a place as clerk in the same store where Sophy Davis is. It was mighty kind o' Mr. Daniels, I think, to offer him the job."

"Well, didn't he take it?"

"Well, partly he did an' partly he did n't, ef you can understand that."

"Sally Martin, what do you mean? A body has to fairly pick a thing out o' you."

"I mean that she told Mr. Daniels he might work fur him half of every day."

"Half a day! An' what's he goin' to do the other half?"

"He's a-goin' to the Bible Seminary the other half-day. She's a-goin' to make a preacher out o' him."

Mrs. Martin had slowly and tortuously worked up to her climax, and she shot forth the last sentence with a jubilant ring. She had well calculated its effects. Sitting back in her chair, she supped her tea complacently as she contemplated her companion's astonishment. Mrs. Smith had completely collapsed into her seat, folded her arms, and closed her eyes. "Laws a massy!" she exclaimed. "What next? Old Tom, drunken Tom, swearin' an' ravin' Tom Brent's boy a preacher!" Then suddenly she opened her eyes and sat up very erect and alert as she broke forth, "Sally Martin, what air you a-tellin' me? It ain't possible. It's ag'in' nature. A panther's cub ain't a-goin' to be a lamb. It's downright wicked, that's what I say."

"An' so says I to Mis' Murphy, them same identical words; says I, 'Mis' Murphy, it's downright wicked. It's a-shamin' of the Lord's holy callin' o' the ministry.'"

"An' does the young scamp pertend to 'a' had a call?"

"No, indeed: he was mighty opposed to it, and so was her husband; but that woman was so set she wouldn't agree to nothin' else. He don't pertend to 'a' heerd no call, 'ceptin' Miss Hester's, an' that was a command. I know it's all true, fur Mis' Murphy, while she wasn't jest a-listenin', lives next door and heerd it all."

And so the two women fell to discussing the question, as they had heard it, pro and con. It was all true, as these gossips had it, that Miss Hester had put into execution her half-expressed determination to make a preacher of Fred. He had heard nothing of it until the day when he rushed in elated over the kindly offer of a place in Mr. Daniels's store. Then his guardian had firmly told him of her plan, and there was a scene.

"You kin jest tell Mr. Daniels that you kin work for him half a day every day, an' that you're a-goin' to put in the rest of your time at the Bible Seminary. I've made all the arrangements."

"But I don't want to be a preacher," the boy had retorted, with some heat. "I'd a good deal rather learn business, and some day start out for myself."

"It ain't what some of us wants to do in this life; it's what the Lord appoints us to; an' it's wicked fur you to rebel."

"I don't know how you can know so much what the Lord means

for me to do. I should think He would give His messages to those who are to do the work."

"That's right, Freddie Brent, sass me, sass me. That's what I've struggled all the best days of my life to raise you fur."

"I'm not sassing you, but—"

"Don't you think, Hester," broke in her husband, "that mebbe there's some truth in what Freddie says? Don't you think the Lord kind o' whispers what He wants people to do in their own ears? Mebbe it wasn't never intended fur Freddie to be a preacher: there's other ways o' doin' good besides a-talkin' from the pulpit."

"I'd be bound fur you, 'Liphalet: it's a shame, you a-goin' ag'in' me, after all I've done to make Freddie material fit for the Lord's use. Jest think what you'll have to answer fur, a-helpin' this unruly boy to shirk his dooty."

"I ain't a-goin' ag'in' you, Hester. You're my wife, an' I 'low 'at your jedgment's purty sound on most things. I ain't a-goin' ag'in' you at all, but—but—I was jest a-wonderin'."

The old man brought out the last words slowly, meditatively. He was "jest a-wonderin'." His wife, though, never wondered.

"Mind you," she went on, "I say to you, Freddie, and to yore uncle 'Liphalet too, ef he upholds you, that it ain't me you're a-rebellin' against. It's yore dooty an' the will o' God that you're a-fightin'. It's easy enough to rebel against man; but do you know what you're a-doin' when you set yourself up against the Almighty? Do you want to do that?"

"Yes," came the boy's answer like a flash. He was stung and irritated into revolt, and a torrent of words poured from his lips unrestrained. "I'm tired of doing right. I'm tired of being good. I'm tired of obeying God—"

"Freddie!" But over the dam the water was flowing with irresistible force. The horror of his guardian's face and the terrible reproach in her voice could not check the boy.

"Everything," he continued, "that I have ever wanted to do since I can remember has been bad, or against my duty, or displeasing to God. Why does He frown on everything I want to do? Why do we always have to be killing our wishes on account of duty? I don't believe it. I hate duty. I hate obedience. I hate everything, and I won't obey—"

"Freddie, be keerful: don't say anything that'll hurt after yore mad spell's over. Don't blaspheme the Lord A'mighty."

'Liphalet Hodges' voice was cool and tender and persuasive. He laid his hand on the boy's shoulder, while his wife sat there motionless, white and rigid with horror.

The old man's words and his gentle touch had a wonderful effect on the boy; they checked his impassioned outburst; but his pent-up heart was too full. He burst into tears and rushed headlong from the house.

For a time he walked aimlessly on, his mind in a tumult of rage. Then he began to come to himself. He saw the people as they passed him. He had eyes again for the street, and he wondered where he was going. He felt an overwhelming desire to talk to some one and to get sympathy, consolation, and perhaps support. But whither should he turn? If 'Liphalet Hodges had been at the old house, his steps would naturally have bent in that direction; but this refuge was no longer his. Then his mind began going over the people whom he knew, and no name so stuck in his fancy as that of Elizabeth. It was a hard struggle. He was bashful. Any other time he would not have done it, but now his great need created in him an intense desperation that made him bold. He turned and retraced his steps toward the Simpson house.

Elizabeth was leaning over the gate. The autumn evening was cool: she had a thin shawl about her shoulders. She was humming a song as Fred came up. His own agitation made her seem irritatingly calm. She opened the gate and made room for him at her side.

"You seem dreadfully warm," she said, "and here I was getting ready to go in because it is so cool."

"I've been walking very fast," he answered, hesitatingly.

"Don't you think you'd better go in, so as not to take cold?"

"Oh, I don't care if I do take cold." The speech sounded rude. Elizabeth looked at him in surprise.

"What's the matter with you?" she asked.

"I'm mad; that's what's the matter."

"Oh, Fred, you shouldn't get mad: you know it's wrong."

He put up his hand as if she had struck him. "Wrong! wrong! It seems I can't hear anything else but that word. Everything is wrong. Don't say any more about it. I don't want to hear the word again."

Elizabeth did not know what to make of his words, so she said nothing, and for a while they stood in strained silence. After a while he said, "Aunt Hester wants me to be a preacher."

"I am so glad to hear that," she returned. "I think you'll make a good one."

"You too!" he exclaimed, resentfully. "Why should I make a good one? Why need I be one at all?"

"Oh, because you're smart, and then you've always been good."

The young man was suddenly filled with disdain. His anger returned. He felt how utterly out of accord he was with every one else. "Don't you think there is anything else required besides being 'smart' and 'good'?" He himself would have blushed at the tone in which he said this, could he have recognised it. "I'm smart because I happened to pass all my examinations. I got through the high school at eighteen: nearly everyone does the same. I'm good because I have never had a chance to be bad: I have never been out of Aunt Hester's sight long enough. Anybody could be good that way."

"But then older people know what is best for us, Fred."

"Why should they? They don't know what's beating inside of us away down here." The boy struck his breast fiercely. "I don't believe they do know half the time what is best, and I don't believe that God intends them to know."

"I wouldn't talk about it, if I were you. I must go in. Won't you come in with me?"

"Not to-night," he replied. "I must be off."

"But papa might give you some advice."

"I've had too much of it now. What I want is room to breathe in once."

"I don't understand you."

"I know you don't; nobody does, or tries to. Go in, Lizzie," he said more calmly. "I don't want you to catch cold, even if I do. Good-night." And he turned away.

The girl stood for a moment looking after him; her eye was moist. Then she pouted, "Fred's real cross to-night," and went in.

It is one of the glaring sarcasms of life to see with what complacency a shallow woman skims the surface of tragedy and thinks that she has sounded the depths.

Fred continued his walk towards home. He was thinking. It ran in him that Elizabeth was a good deal of a fool; and then he felt horrified with himself for thinking it. It did not occur to him that the hard conditions through which he had come had made him mentally and spiritually older than the girl. He was thinking of his position, how perfectly alone he stood. Most of the people whom he knew would see only blind obstinacy in his refusal to be a minister. But were one's inclinations nothing? Was there really nothing in the "call" to preach? So he pondered as he walked, and more and more the hopelessness of his predicament became revealed to him. All his life had been moulded by this one woman's hands. Would not revolt now say to the world, "I am grown now; I do not need this woman who has toiled. I can disobey her with impunity; I will do so."

He went home, and before going in leaned his head long upon the gate and thought. A listless calm had succeeded his storm of passion. He went in and to bed.

At breakfast he seemed almost cheerful, while Mr. Hodges was subdued. His wife had taken refuge in an attitude of injured silence.

"Aunt Hester," said the young man, apparently without effort, "I was wrong yesterday; I am sorry. I will do whatever you say, even to being a preacher." Something came up in his throat and choked him as he saw a brightness come into the face and eyes of his beloved "Uncle 'Liph," but it grew hard and bitter there as Mrs. Hodges replied, "Well, I'm glad the Lord has showed you the errors of your way an' brought you around to a sense o' your dooty to Him an' to me."

Poor, blind, conceited humanity! Interpreters of God, indeed! We reduce the Deity to vulgar fractions. We place our own little ambitions and inclinations before a shrine, and label them "divine messages." We set up our Delphian tripod, and we are the priest and oracles. We despise the plans of Nature's Ruler and substitute our own. With our short sight we affect to take a comprehensive view of eternity. Our horizon is the universe. We spy on the Divine and try to surprise His secrets, or to sneak into His confidence by stealth. We make God the eternal a puppet. We measure infinity with a foot-rule.

CHAPTER X

When Fate is fighting with all her might against a human soul, the greatest victory that the soul can win is to reconcile itself to the unpleasant, which is never quite so unpleasant afterwards. Upon this principle Frederick Brent acted instinctively. What with work and study and contact with his fellow-students, he found the seminary not so bad a place, after all. Indeed, he began to take a sort of pleasure in his pursuits. The spirit of healthy competition in the school whetted his mind and made him forgetful of many annoyances from without. When some fellow-salesman at the store gibed at him for being a parson, it hurt him; but the wound was healed and he was compensated when in debate he triumphed over the crack speaker of his class. It was a part of his training to do earnestly and thoroughly what he had to do, even though it was distasteful, and it was not long before he was spoken of as one of the most promising members of the school.

Notwithstanding its steady growth toward citydom, Dexter retained many of the traditions of its earlier and smaller days. Among them was that of making the church the centre of its social and public life. For this reason the young student came in for much attention on account of his standing in the religious college. Another cause which elicited the praise and congratulations of his friends was his extreme youth. That community which could send out a "boy preacher" always deemed itself particularly favoured by Providence. Dexter was no exception, and it had already begun to bestow the appellation upon young Brent, much to his disgust. He knew the species and detested it. It was mostly composed of ignorant and hypocritical young prigs, in whom their friends had seemed to see some especial merit and had forthwith hoisted them into a position that was as foolish as it was distasteful. They were hailed as youthful prodigies and exploited around the country like a patent medicine or a side-show. What is remarkable at eighteen is not so striking at twenty-eight. So when their extreme youth was no longer a cause for surprise, the boy preachers settled down into every-day dullness, with nothing except the memory of a flimsy fame to compensate the congregations they bored.

Against this Frederick Brent fought with all his strength. He refused invitation after invitation to "talk" or "exhort," on the plea that he wished to be fully prepared for his work before entering upon it.

But his success at school militated against him, for the fame of his oratorical powers was gradually but surely leaking out. The faculty recognised and commended it, so he could not hope long to hide behind his plea, although he dreaded the day when it would no longer serve his purpose.

Some of the "older heads" accused him of an unwarranted fear, of cowardice even, and an attempt to shirk his evident duty. The truth of it was that these same people wanted to hear him and then attack his manner or his doctrine. They could not, would not forget that he was the son of old Tom Brent, the drunkard, and of the terrible, the unspeakable Margaret, his wife. They could not forget that he was born and lived the first years of his life on the "mean" street, when it was a mean street; and when any obstinate old fossil was told of the youth's promise, he would shake his head, as who should say, "What good can come out of that Nazareth?"

But the young man went his way and heeded them not. He knew what they were saying. He knew what they were thinking, even when they held his hand and smiled upon him, and it filled him with a spirit of distrust and resentment, though it put him bravely on his mettle. While he was a man, and in the main manly, sometimes he was roused to an anger almost childish; then, although he did not want to be a preacher at all, he wished and even prayed to become a great one, just to convince the old fools who shook their heads over him. To his ears had crept, as such tales will creep, some of the stories of his parents' lives, and, while he pitied his mother, there was a great fierceness in his heart against his father.

But as in the old days when Miss Prime's discipline would have turned all within him to hardness and bitterness Eliphalet Hodges stood between him and despair, so now in this crucial time Elizabeth was a softening influence in his life.

As the days came and went, he had continued to go to see her ever since the night when he had stood with her at the gate and felt the bitterness of her lack of sympathy; but all that had passed now, and unconsciously they had grown nearer to each other. There had been a tacit understanding between them until just a few weeks before. It was on a warm spring evening: he had just passed through her gate and started towards the house, when the opening chords of the piano struck on his ear through the opened window and arrested him. Elizabeth had a pleasant little voice, with a good deal of natural pathos in it. As the minister's daughter, the scope of her songs was properly, according to Dexter, rather limited, but that evening she was singing softly to herself a love-song. The words were these:

> *If Death should claim me for her own to-day,*
>   *And softly I should falter from your side,*
> *Oh, tell me, loved one, would my memory stay,*
>   *And would my image in your heart abide?*
> *Or should I be as some forgotten dream,*
>   *That lives its little space, then fades entire?*
> *Should Time send o'er you its relentless stream,*
>   *To cool your heart, and quench for aye love's fire?*
>
> *I would not for the world, love, give you pain,*
>   *Or ever compass what would cause you grief;*
> *And oh, how well I know that tears are vain!*
>   *But love is sweet, my dear, and life is brief;*
> *So, if some day before you I should go*
>   *Beyond the sound and sight of song and sea,*
> *'T would give my spirit stronger wings to know*
>   *That you remembered still and wept for me.*

She was alone in the room. The song was hardly finished when Brent stepped through the window and laid his hand over hers where they rested on the keys.

"Why do you sing like that, Elizabeth?" he said, tremulously.

She blushed and lowered her eyes beneath his gaze, as if she already knew the words that were on his lips, or feared that her soul lay too bare before him.

"Why do you think of death?" he asked again, imprisoning her hands.

"It was only my mood," she faltered. "I was thinking, and I thought of the song, and I just sang it."

"Were you thinking of any one in particular, Lizzie?"

Her head drooped lower until her face was hidden, but she did not answer. A strange boldness had come to him. He went on: "I listened as you were singing, and it seemed as if every word was meant for me, Lizzie. It may sound foolish, but I—I love you. Won't you look at me and tell me that I am right in thinking you love me?" She half raised her face to his and murmured one word. In it were volumes; he bent down and kissed her. It was the first time he had ever kissed a girl. He did it almost fearfully. It was a kiss in which reverence struggled with passion.

"You are to be my little sweetheart now, and I am to be in your thoughts hereafter when you sing; only we don't want any more such songs as this one. I don't want to 'remember still and weep for you,' I want to have you always by me and work for you. Won't you let me?"

Elizabeth found her tongue for a moment only, but that was enough for her lover. A happy light gleamed in his eyes: his face glowed. He was transfigured. Love does so much for a man.

From that time forward, when he was harassed by cares and trouble, he sought out Elizabeth, and, even though he could seldom tell her all that was in his heart, he found relief in her presence. He did not often speak of his trials to her, for, in spite of his love for her, he felt that she could not understand; but the pleasure he found in her company put sweetness into his life and made his burdens easier to bear.

Only once had a little shadow come between them, and the fact that so little a thing could have made a shadow shows in what a narrow, constrained atmosphere the two young people lived. Young Brent still had his half-day position in the store, and when the employees of a rival establishment challenged Daniels's clerks to a game of baseball, he was duly chosen as one of the men to uphold the honour of their house upon the diamond.

The young man was not fossilised. He had strength and the capacity for enjoyment, so he accepted without a thought of wrong. The Saturday came, the game was played. Fred Brent took part, and thereby brought a hornets' nest about his ears. It would scarcely have been so bad, but the young man entered the game with all the zest and earnestness of his intense nature, and several times by brilliant playing saved his side from defeat. In consequence, his name was in the mouth of every one who had seen or heard of the contest.

He was going home that evening, feeling pleased and satisfied with himself, when he thought he would drop in a moment on the way and see Elizabeth. He had hardly got into the house before he saw from her manner that something was wrong, and he wondered what it could be. He soon learned. It is only praise that is slow.

"Oh, Fred," said the girl, reproachfully, "is it true that you have been playing baseball?"

"Baseball, yes; what of it? What are you looking so horrified about?"

"Did you think it was right for you, in your position, to play?"

"If I had thought it was wrong I assuredly should not have played," the young man returned.

"Everybody is talking about it, and father says he thinks you have disgraced your calling."

"Disgraced my calling by playing an innocent game?"

"But father thinks it is a shame for a man who is preparing to do such work as yours to have people talking about him as a mere ball-player."

The blood mounted in hot surges to the young man's face. He felt like saying, "Your father be hanged," but he controlled his anger, and said, quietly, "Elizabeth, don't you ever think for yourself?"

"I suppose I do, Fred, but I have been brought up to respect what my elders think and say."

"Don't you think that they, as well as we, can be narrow and mistaken?"

"It is not for me to judge them. My part is to obey."

"You have learned an excellent lesson," he returned, bitterly. "That is just the thing: 'obey, obey.' Well, I will. I will be a stick, a dolt. I will be as unlike what God intended me to be as possible. I will be just what your father and Aunt Hester and you want me to be. I will let them think for me and save my soul. I am too much an imbecile to attempt to work out my own salvation. No, Elizabeth, I will not play ball any more. I can imagine the horrified commotion it caused among the angels when they looked down and saw me pitching. When I get back to school I shall look up the four Gospels' views on ball-playing."

"Fred, I don't like you when you talk that way."

"I won't do that any more, either." He rose abruptly. "Good-bye, Elizabeth. I am off." He was afraid to stay, lest more bitter words should come to his lips.

"Good-bye, Fred," she said. "I hope you understand."

The young man wondered as he walked homeward if the girl he had chosen was not a little bit prim. Then he thought of her father, and said to himself, even as people would have said of himself, "How can she help it, with such a father?"

All his brightness had been dashed. He was irritated because the thing was so small, so utterly absurd. It was like the sting of a miserable little insect,—just enough to smart, and not enough to need a strong remedy. The news of the game had also preceded him home, and his guardian's opinion of the propriety of his action did not tend to soothe his mind. Mrs. Hodges forcibly expressed herself as follows: "I put baseball-playin' right down with dancin' and sich like. It ain't no fittin' occupation for any one that's a-goin' into the ministry. It's idleness, to begin with; it's a-wastin' the precious time that's been given us for a better use. A young man that's goin' to minister to people's souls ought to be consecrated to the work before he begins it. Who ever heerd tell of Jesus playin' baseball?"

Among a certain class of debaters such an argument is always supposed to be clinching, unanswerable, final. But Mr. Hodges raised his voice in protest. "I ain't a-goin' to keep still no longer. I don't believe the boy's done a bit o' harm. There's lots of things the Lord didn't do that He didn't forbid human bein's to do. We ain't none of us divine, but you mark my words, Freddie, an' I say it right here so's yore aunt Hester can hear me too, you mark my words: ef you never do nothin' worse than what you've been a-doin' to-day, it'll be mighty easy for you to read yore title clear to mansions in the skies."

"Omph huh, 'Liphalet, there ain't nothin' so easy as talkin' when Satin's a-promptin' you."

"There you go, Hester, there you go ag'in, a-pattin' the devil on the back. I 'low the Old Boy must be tickled to death with all the compliments Christian people give him."

"A body'd about as well be complimentin' the devil as to be a-countenancin' his works, as you air."

The old man stopped with a piece half-way to his mouth. "Now jest listen at that! Hester Prime, ain't you ashamed of yoreself? Me a-countenancin' wrong! Sayin' that to me, an' me ol' enough to be—to be—well, I'm your husband, anyway."

In times of excitement he was apt to forget this fact for the instant and give his wife her maiden name, as if all that was sharp in her belonged to that prenuptial period. But this storm relieved the atmosphere of its tension. Mrs. Hodges felt better for having spoken her mind, and Mr. Hodges for having answered, while the young man was relieved by the championship of his elder, and so the storm blew over. It was several days before Brent saw Elizabeth again; but, thanks to favouring winds, the sky had also cleared in that direction.

It was through such petty calms and storms that Fred passed the days and weeks of his first year at the seminary. Some of them were small annoyances, to be sure, but he felt them deeply, and the sting of them rankled. It is not to be supposed, because there was no specific outburst, that he was entirely at rest. Vesuvius had slumbered long before Pompeii's direful day. His mind was often in revolt, but he kept it to himself or confided it to only one friend. This friend was a fellow-student at the seminary, a man older than Fred by some years. He had first begun a literary career, but had renounced it for the ministry. Even to him Fred would not commit himself until, near the end of the year, Taylor declared his intention of now renouncing the study of theology for his old pursuits. Then Brent's longing to be free likewise drew his story from his lips.

Taylor listened to him with the air of one who had been through it all and could sympathise. Then he surprised his friend by saying, "Don't be a fool, Brent. It's all very nice and easy to talk about striking out for one's self, and all that. I've been through it all myself. My advice to you is, stay here, go through the academic discipline, and be a parson. Get into a rut if you will, for some ruts are safe. When we are buried deep, they keep us from toppling over. This may be a sort of weak philosophy I am trying to teach you, but it is the happiest. If I can save any man from self-delusion, I want to do it. I'll tell you why. When I was at school some fool put it into my head that I could write. I hardly know how it came about. I began scribbling of my own accord and for my own amusement. Sometimes I showed the things to my friend, who was a fool: he bade me keep on, saying that I had talent. I didn't believe it at first. But when a fellow keeps dinging at another with one remark, after a while he grows to believe it, especially when it is pleasant. It is vastly easy to believe what we want to believe. So I came to think that I could write, and my soul was fired with the ambition to make a name for myself in literature. When I should have been turning Virgil into English for class-room, I was turning out more or less deformed verse of my own, or rapt in the contemplation of some plot for story or play. But somehow I got through school without a decided flunk. In the mean time some of my lines had found their way into print, and the little cheques I received for them had set my head buzzing with dreams of wealth to be made by my pen. If we could only pass the pitfalls of that dreaming age of youth, most of us would get along fairly well in this matter-of-fact old world. But we are likely to follow blindly the leadings of our dreams until we run our heads smack into a corner-post of reality. Then we awaken, but in most cases too late.

"I am glad to say that my father had the good sense to discourage my aspirations. He wanted me to take a profession. But, elated by the applause of my friends, I scorned the idea. What, mew my talents up in a courtroom or a hospital? Never! It makes me sick when I look back upon it and see what a fool I was. I settled down at home and began writing. Lots of things came back from periodicals to which I sent them; but I had been told that this was the common lot of all writers, and I plodded on. A few things sold, just enough to keep my hopes in a state of unstable equilibrium.

"Well, it's no use to tell you how I went on in that way for four years, clinging and losing hold, standing and slipping, seeing the prize recede just as I seemed to grasp it. Then came the awakening. I saw that it would have been better just to go on and do the conventional thing. I found this out too late, and I came here to try to remedy it, but I can't. No one can. You get your mind into a condition where the ordinary routine of study is an impossibility, and you cannot go back and take up the train you have laid, so you keep struggling on wasting your energy, hoping against hope. Then suddenly you find out that you are and can be only third- or at best second-rate. God, what a discovery it is! How you try to fight it off until the last moment! But it comes upon you surely and crushingly, and, cut, bruised, wounded, you slip away from the face of the world. If you are a brave man, you say boldly to yourself, 'I will eke out an existence in some humble way,' and you go away to a life of longing and regret. If you are a coward, you either leap over the parapets of life to hell, or go creeping back and fall at the feet of the thing that has damned you, willing to be third-rate, anything; for you are stung with the poison that never leaves your blood. So it has been with me: even when I found that I must choose a calling, I chose the one that gave me most time to nurse the serpent that had stung me."

Taylor ceased speaking, and looked a little ashamed of his vehemence.

"This is your story," said Brent; "but men differ and conditions differ. I will accept all the misery, all the pain and defeat you have suffered, to be free to choose my own course."

Taylor threw up his hands with a deprecatory gesture. "There," he said; "it is always so. I might as well have talked to the wind."

So the fitful calms and Elizabeth's love had not cured Frederick Brent's heart of its one eating disease, the desire for freedom.

CHAPTER XI

I t was not until early in Brent's second year at the Bible Seminary that he was compelled to go through the ordeal he so much dreaded, that of filling a city pulpit. The Dexterites had been wont to complain that since the advent among them of the theological school their churches had been turned into recitation-rooms for the raw students; but of "old Tom Brent's boy," as they still called him, they could never make this complaint. So, as humanity loves to grumble, the congregations began to find fault because he did not do as his fellows did.

The rumours of his prowess in the class-room and his eloquence in the society hall had not abated, and the curiosity of his fellow-townsmen had been whetted to a point where endurance was no longer possible. Indeed, it is open to question whether it was not by connivance of the minister himself, backed by his trustees on one side and the college authorities on the other, that Brent was finally deputed to supply the place of the Rev. Mr. Simpson, who was affected by an indisposition, fancied, pretended, or otherwise.

The news struck the young man like a thunderbolt, albeit he had been expecting it. He attempted to make his usual excuse, but the kindly old professor who had notified him smiled into his face, and, patting his shoulder, said, "It's no use, Brent. I'd go and make the best of it; they're bound to have you. I understand your diffidence in the matter, and, knowing how well you stand in class, it does credit to your modesty."

The old man passed on. He said he understood, but in his heart the young student standing there helpless, hopeless, knew that he did not understand, that he could not. Only he himself could perceive it in all the trying horror of its details. Only he himself knew fully or could know what the event involved,—that when he arose to preach, to nine-tenths of the congregation he would not be Frederick Brent, student, but "old Tom Brent's boy." He recoiled from the thought.

Many a fireside saint has said, "Why did not Savonarola tempt the hot ploughshares? God would not have let them burn him." Faith is a beautiful thing. But Savonarola had the ploughshares at his feet. The children of Israel stepped into the Red Sea before the waters parted, but then Moses was with them, and, what was more, Pharaoh was behind them.

At home, the intelligence of what Brent was to do was received in different manner by Mrs. Hodges and her husband. The good lady launched immediately into a lecture on the duty that was placed in his hands; but Eliphalet was silent as they sat at the table. He said nothing until after supper was over, and then he whispered to his young friend as he started to his room, "I know jest how you feel, Freddie. It seems that I oughtn't to call you that now; but I 'low you'll allus be 'Freddie' to me."

"Don't ever call me anything else, if you please, Uncle 'Liph," said the young man, pressing Eliphalet's hand.

"I think I kin understand you better than most people," Mr. Hodges went on; "an' I know it ain't no easy task that you've got before you."

"You've always understood me better than any one, and—and I wish you knew what it has meant to me, and that I could thank you somehow."

"'Sh, my boy. It's thanks enough to hear them words from you. Now you jest calm yoreself, an' when Sunday comes—I don't know as I'd ought to say it this way, but I mean it all in a Christian sperrit—when Sunday comes, Freddie, my boy, you jest go in an' give 'em fits."

The two parted with another pressure of the hand, and it must be confessed that the old man looked a little bit sheepish when his wife hoped he had been giving Fred good advice.

"You don't reckon, Hester, that I'd give him any other kind, do you?"

"Not intentionally, 'Liphalet; but when it comes to advice, there's p'ints o' view." Mrs. Hodges seemed suspicious of her husband's capabilities as an adviser.

"There's some times when people'd a good deal ruther have sympathy than advice."

"An' I reckon, 'cordin' to yore way o' thinkin' this is one o' them. Well, I intend to try to do my dooty in this matter, as I've tried to do it all along."

72

"Hester, yore dooty'll kill you yit. It's a wonder you don't git tired a-lookin' it in the face."

"I ain't a-goin' to shirk it, jest to live in pleasure an' ease."

"No need o' shirkin', Hester, no need o' shirkin'; but they's some people that wouldn't be content without rowin' down stream."

"An' then, mind you, 'Liphalet, I ain't a-exchangin' words with you, fur that's idleness, but there's others, that wouldn't row up stream, but 'ud wait an' hope fur a wind to push 'em." These impersonalities were as near "spatting" as Mr. and Mrs. Hodges ever got.

Through all the community that clustered about Mr. Simpson's church and drew its thoughts, ideas, and subjects of gossip therefrom, ran like wildfire the news that at last they were to have a chance to judge of young Brent's merits for themselves. It caused a stir among old and young, and in the days preceding the memorable Sunday little else was talked of.

When it reached the ears of old Dan'l Hastings, who limped around now upon two canes, but was as acrimonious as ever, he exclaimed, tapping the ground with one of his sticks for emphasis, "What! that young Brent preachin' in our church, in our minister's pulpit! It's a shame,—an' he the born son of old Tom Brent, that all the town knows was the worst sinner hereabouts. I ain't a-goin' to go; I ain't a-goin' to go."

"Don't you be afeared to go, Dan'l: there ain't no danger that his docterns air a-goin' to be as strong as his father's whisky," said his old enemy.

"Oh, it's fur the likes o' you, Thomas Donaldson, to be a-talkin' o' docterns an' whisky in the same breath. You never did have no reverence," said the old man, testily.

"An' yet, Dan'l, I've found docterns an' whisky give out by the same breath."

Mr. Hastings did not think it necessary to notice this remark. He went on with his tirade against the prospective "supply:" "Why can't Elder Simpson preach hisself, I'd like to know, instead o' puttin' up that young upstart to talk to his betters? Why, I mind the time that that boy had to be took out o' church by the hand fur laffin' at me,— at me, mind you," the old man repeated, shaking his stick; "laffin' at me when I was expoundin' the word."

"That's ter'ble, Dan'l; fur, as fur as I kin ricollec', when you're a-expoundin' the word it ain't no laffin' matter."

"I tell you, Thomas Donaldson, the world's a-goin' down hill fast: but I ain't a-goin' to help it along. I ain't a-goin' to hear that Brent boy preach."

This declaration, however, did not prevent the venerable Dan'l from being early in his seat on the following Sunday morning, sternly, uncompromisingly critical.

As might have been expected, the church was crowded. Friends, enemies, and the merely curious filled the seats and blocked the aisles. The chapel had been greatly enlarged to accommodate its growing congregation, but on this day it was totally inadequate to hold the people who flocked to its doors.

The Rev. Mr. Simpson was so far recovered from his indisposition as to be able to be present and assist at the service. Elizabeth was there, looking proud and happy and anxious. Mrs. Hodges was in her accustomed place on the ladies' side of the pulpit. She had put new strings to her bonnet in honour of the occasion. Her face wore a look of great severity. An unregenerate wag in the back part of the church pointed her out to his companions and remarked that she looked as if she'd spank the preacher if he didn't do well. "Poor fellow, if he sees that face he'll break down, sure." Opposite, in the "amen corner," the countenance of the good Eliphalet was a study in changing expressions. It was alternately possessed by fear, doubt, anxiety, and exultation.

Sophy Davis sat in a front seat, spick and span in a new dress, which might have been made for the occasion. People said that she was making eyes at her young fellow-salesman, though she was older than he. Mrs. Martin and her friend whispered together a little farther back.

A short time before the service began, Brent entered by a side door near the pulpit and ascended to his place. His entrance caused a marked sensation. His appearance was impressive. The youthful face was white and almost rigid in its lines. "Scared to death," was the mental note of a good many who saw him. But his step was firm. As Elizabeth looked at him, she felt proud that such a man loved her. He was not handsome. His features were irregular, but his eyes were clear and fearless. If a certain cowardice had held him back from this ordeal, it was surely not because he trembled for himself. The life he had lived and the battles he had fought had given a compression to his lips that corrected a natural tendency to weakness in his mouth.

His head was set squarely on his broad shoulders. He was above medium height, but not loosely framed. He looked the embodiment of strength.

"He ain't a bit like his father," said some one.

"He's like his father was in his best days," replied another.

"He don't look like he's over-pleased with the business. They say he didn't want to come."

"Well, I guess it's purty resky work gittin' up to speak before all these people that's knowed him all his life, an' know where an' what he come from."

"They say, too, that he's some pumpkins out at the college."

"I 'ain't much faith in these school-made preachers; but we'll soon see what he kin do in the pulpit. We've heerd preachers, an' we kin compare."

"That's so: we've heerd some preachers in our day. He must toe the mark. He may be all right at college, but he's in a pulpit now that has held preachers fur shore. A pebble's all right among pebbles, but it looks mighty small 'longside o' boulders. He's preachin' before people now. Why, Brother Simpson himself never would 'a' got a special dispensation to hold the church all these years, ef it hadn't been fur the people backin' him up an' Conference was afraid they'd leave the connection."

"Well, ef this boy is anything, Lord only knows where he gets it, fur everybody knows—"

"'Sh!"

The buzz which had attended the young speaker's entrance subsided as Mr. Simpson rose and gave out the hymn. That finished, he ran his eyes over the front seats of the assembly and then said, "Brother Hastings, lead us in prayer."

The old man paused for an instant as if surprised, and then got slowly to his knees. It was a strange selection, but we have seen that this particular parson was capable of doing strange things. In the course of a supplication of some fifteen minutes' duration, Brother Hastings managed to vent his spleen upon the people and to pay the Lord a few clumsy compliments. During the usual special blessing which is asked upon the preacher of the hour, he prayed, "O Lord, let not the rarin' horses of his youth run away with Thy chariot of eternal truth. Lord, cool his head and warm his heart and settle him firm. Grant that he may fully realise where he's a-standin' at, an' who he's a-speakin' to. Do Thou not let him speak, but speak through him, that Thy gospel may be preached to-day as Thy prophets of old preached it."

Throughout the prayer, but one thought was running through Frederick Brent's mind, and his heart was crying in its anguish, "Oh, my God, my God, why do they hound me so?"

It is a terrible thing, this first effort before the home people, especially when home has not been kind.

When he arose to meet the people's eyes, his face was haggard and he felt weak. But unflinchingly he swept his eyes over the crowd, and that instant's glance brought before him all the panorama of the past years. There before him was the sneaking Billy Tompkins, now grown to the maturity of being called "Bill." Then there was Dan'l Hastings. Oh, that night, years ago, when he had been marched up the aisle with crimson face! In one brief second he lived it all over again, the shame, the disgrace, the misery of it. There, severe, critical, expectant, sat his guardian, the master-hand who had manipulated all the machinery of his life. All this passed through his mind in a flash, as he stood there facing the people. His face changed. The haggard look passed away. His eyes kindled, his cheeks mantled. Even in the pulpit, even in the house of God, about to speak His word, the blood sped hotly through his veins, and anger burned at his heart. But he crushed down his feelings for the moment, and began in a clear ringing voice, "Judge not, that ye be not judged. For with what judgment ye judge, ye shall be judged, and with what measure ye mete, it shall be measured to you again." The lesson he drew from the words was God's recognition of the fallibility of human judgment, and the self-condemnation brought about by ignoring the prohibition in the text. By an effort, he spoke deliberately at first, but the fire in his heart came out more and more in his words as he progressed. "Blinded by our own prejudices," he said, "circumscribed by our own ignorance, we dare to set ourselves up as censors of our fellow-men. Unable to see the whole chain of life which God has forged, we take a single link and say that it is faulty. Too narrow to see His broad plan, we take a patch of it and say, 'This is not good.' There is One who works even through evil that good may come, but we take the sin of our brother, and, without seeing or knowing what went before it or shall come after, condemn him. What false, blind, petty judges we are! You women who are condemning your fallen sisters, you men who are execrating your sinful brothers, if Christ to-day were to command, 'Let him who is without sin cast the first stone,' look into your own hearts and answer me, how many of you would dare to lift a hand? How many of you have taken the beam out of your own eye before attempting to pluck the mote out of your brother's? O ye pharisaical ones, who stand in the public places and thank God that you are not as other men, beware, beware. The condemnation that surely and inevitably shall fall upon you is not the judgment of Jesus Christ. It is not the sentence of the Father. It is your own self-condemnation, without charity, without forbearance, without love; 'for with what judgment ye judge ye shall be judged.'

"Stand by the wayside if you will. Draw aside your skirts in the vainglory of self-righteousness from the passing multitude. Say to each other, if you will, 'This woman is a sinner: this man is a criminal.' Close your eyes against their acts of repentance, harden your hearts against their pleas for forgiveness, withhold mercy and pardon and charity; but I tell you of One who has exalted charity into the highest and best of virtues. I bring you the message of One whose judgment is tempered by divine love. He is seeing you. He is hearing you. Over the parapets of high heaven the gentle Father leans waiting to take into His soul any breath of human love or charity which floats up to Him from this sin-parched world. What have you done to merit His approval? Have you been kind, or have you been hard? Have you been gentle, or have you been harsh? Have you been charitable, or have you hunted out all the evil and closed your eyes to all the good? You have forgotten, O ye of little faith, you have forgotten, you without charity in your hearts, and you who claim to follow Christ and yet have no love for your fellows,—you have forgotten that God is a God of wrath as well as of love; that Christ hath anger as well as pity; that He who holds the hyssop of divine mercy holds also the scourge of divine indignation. You have forgotten that the lash you so love to wield over your brother's back shall be laid upon your own by Him who whipped the money-changers from His temple. Listen! The day shall come when the condemnation you are accumulating against yourselves shall overwhelm you. Stop trying to steal the prerogative of heaven. Judge not. God only is just!"

The silence throughout the sermon was intense. During the closing words which have been quoted, it was like a presence in the chapel. The voice of the preacher rang out like a clarion. His eyes looked before him as if he saw into the future. His hand was uplifted as if he would call down upon them the very judgment which he predicted.

Without more words he sat down. No one moved or spoke for an instant. Dan'l Hastings let his cane fall upon the floor. It echoed through the silent place with a crash. Some of the women started and half cried out; but the spell was now partly broken. Mr. Simpson suddenly remembered to pray, and the gossips forgot to whisper when their heads were bowed. There were some pale faces in the crowd, and some which the galling of tears had made red. There was in the atmosphere something of the same tense silence that follows a terrific thunder-clap. And so the service ended, and the people filed out of church silent still. Some few remained behind to shake the preacher's hand, but as soon as the benediction was over he hurried out the side door, and, before any one could intercept him, was on his way home. But he left a willing substitute. Mrs. Hodges accepted all his congratulations with complacent condescension.

"Dan'l," said Thomas Donaldson, as he helped the old man down the church steps, "I was mistaken about the docterns an' the whisky. It was stronger an' better, because it was the pure stuff."

"I 'ain't got a word to say," said Dan'l, "'ceptin' that a good deal of it was jest sass." But he kept mumbling to himself as he hobbled along, "Jedge not, fur you're a-pilin' up sentences on yoreself. I never thought of it that way before; no, I never."

Brent did not come out of his room to dinner that afternoon. Mrs. Hodges was for calling him, but the old man objected. "No, Hester," he said, "Freddie jest wants to be let alone. He's a-feelin' now."

"But, 'Liphalet, he ought to know how nice people talked about his sermon. I tell you that was my kind o' doctern. It's wonderful how a child will learn."

Notwithstanding his belief that his young friend wanted to be left alone, the old man slipped into his room later on with a cup of tea. The young man sat before the table, his head buried in his hands. Eliphalet set the cup and saucer down and turned to go, but he paused at the door and said, "Thank the Lord fur the way you give it to 'em, Freddie. It was worth a dollar." He would have hurried out, but the young man sprang up and seized his hand, exclaiming, "It was wrong, Uncle 'Liph, it was wrong of me. I saw them sitting about me like jackals waiting for their prey; I remembered all that I had been and all that I was; I knew what they were thinking, and I was angry, angry. God forgive me! That sermon was preached from as hot a heart as ever did murder."

The old man stroked the young one's hair as he would a child's. "Never mind," he said. "It don't matter what you felt. That's between you an' Him. I only know what you said, an' that's all I care about. Didn't you speak about the Lord a-whippin' the money-changers from the temple? Ain't lots o' them worse than the money-changers? Wasn't Christ divine? Ain't you human? Would a body expect you to feel less'n He did? Huh! jest don't you worry; remember that you didn't hit a head that wasn't in striking distance." And the old man pressed the boy back into his chair and slipped out.

CHAPTER XII

Beside an absolute refusal again to supply, Brent made no sign of the rebellion which was in him, and his second year slipped quickly and uneventfully away. He went to and from his duties silent and self-contained. He did not confide in Mr. Hodges, because his guardian seemed to grow more and more jealous of their friendship. He could not confide in Elizabeth, on account of a growing conviction that she did not fully sympathise with him. But his real feelings may be gathered from a letter which he wrote to his friend Taylor some two months after the events recorded in the last chapter.

"My dear Taylor," it ran, "time and again I have told myself that I would write you a line, keeping you in touch, as I promised, with my progress. Many times have I thought of our last talk together, and still I think as I thought then—that, in spite of all your disadvantages and your defeats, you have the best of it. When you fail, it is your own failure, and you bear down with you only your own hopes and struggles and ideals. If I fail, there falls with me all the framework of pride and anxiety that has so long pushed me forward and held me up. For my own failure I should not sorrow: my concern would be for the one who has so carefully shaped me after a pattern of her own. However else one may feel, one must be fair to the ambitions of others, even though one is the mere material that is heated and beaten into form on the anvil of another's will. But I am ripe for revolt. The devil is in me,—a restrained, quiet, well-appearing devil, but all the more terrible for that.

"I have at last supplied one of the pulpits here, that of my own church. The Rev. Mr. Simpson was afflicted with a convenient and adaptable indisposition which would not allow him to preach, and I was deputed to fill his place. I knew what a trial it would be, and had carefully written out my sermon, but I am afraid I did not adhere very strictly to the manuscript. I think I lost my head. I know I lost my temper. But the sermon was a nine days' wonder, and I have had to refuse a dozen subsequent offers to supply. It is all very sordid and sickening and theatrical. The good old Lowry tried to show me that it was my duty and for my good, but I have set my foot down not to supply again, and so they let me alone now.

"It seems to me that that one sermon forged a chain which holds me in a position that I hate. It is a public declaration that I am or mean to be a preacher, and I must either adhere to it or break desperately away. Do you know, I feel myself to be an arrant coward. If I had half the strength that you have, I should have been out of it long ago; but the habit of obedience grows strong upon a man.

"There is but one crowning act to be added to this drama of deceit and infamy,—my ordination. I know how all the other fellows are looking forward to it, and how, according to all the prescribed canons, I should view the momentous day; but I am I. Have you ever had one of those dreams where a huge octopus approaches you slowly but certainly, enfolding you in his arms and twining his horrid tentacles about your helpless form? What an agony of dread you feel! You try to move or cry out, but you cannot, and the arms begin to embrace you and draw you towards the great body. Just so I feel about the day of the ceremony that shall take me into the body of which I was never destined to be a member.

"Are you living in a garret? Are you subsisting on a crust? Happy, happy fellow! But, thank God, the ordination does not take place until next year, and perhaps in that time I may find some means of escape. If I do not, I know that I shall have your sympathy; but don't express it. Ever sincerely yours, Brent."

But the year was passing, and nothing happened to release him. He found himself being pushed forward at the next term with unusual rapidity, but he did not mind it; the work rather gave him relief from more unpleasant thoughts. He went at it with eagerness and mastered it with ease. His fellow-students looked on him with envy, but he went on his way unheeding and worked for the very love of being active, until one day he understood.

It was nearing the end of the term when a fellow-student remarked to him, "Well, Brent, it isn't every man that could have done it, but you'll get your reward in a month or so now."

"What do you mean?" asked Brent. "Done what?"

"Now don't be modest," rejoined the other; "I am really glad to see you do it. I have no envy."

"Really, Barker, I don't understand you."

"Why, I mean you are finishing two years in one."

"Oh, pshaw! it will hardly amount to that."

"Oh, well, you will get in with the senior class men."

"Get in with the senior class!"

"It will be kind of nice, a year before your time, to be standing in the way of any appointive plums that may happen to fall; and then you don't have to go miles away from home before you can be made a full-fledged shepherd. Well, here is my hand on it anyway."

Brent took the proffered hand in an almost dazed condition. It had all suddenly flashed across his mind, the reason for his haste and his added work. What a blind fool he had been!

The Church Conference met at Dexter that year, and they had hurried him through in order that he might be ready for ordination thereat.

Alleging illness as an excuse, he did not appear at recitation that day. The shock had come too suddenly for him. Was he thus to be entrapped? Could he do nothing? He felt that ordination would bind him for ever to the distasteful work. He had only a month in which to prevent it. He would do it. From that day he tried to fall gradually back in his work; but it was too late; the good record which he had unwittingly piled up carried him through, *nolens volens*.

The week before Conference met, Frederick Brent, residing at Dexter, by special request of the faculty, was presented as a candidate for ordination. Even his enemies in the community said, "Surely there is something in that boy."

Mrs. Hester Hodges was delighted. She presented him with his ordination suit, and altogether displayed a pride and pleasure that almost reconciled the young man to his fate. In the days immediately preceding the event she was almost tender with him, and if he had been strong enough to make a resolve inimical to her hopes, the disappointment which he knew failure would bring to her would have greatly weakened it.

Now, Conference is a great event in the circles of that sect of which Cory Chapel was a star congregation, and the town where it convenes, or "sets," as the popular phrase goes, is an honoured place. It takes upon itself an air of unusual bustle. There is a great deal of house-cleaning, hanging of curtains, and laying of carpets, just prior to the time. People from the rural parts about come into town and settle for the week. Ministers and lay delegates from all the churches in the district, comprising perhaps half of a large State or parts of two, come and are quartered upon the local members of the connection. For two weeks beforehand the general question that passes from one housewife to another is, "How many and whom are you going to take?" Many are the heartburnings and jealousies aroused by the disposition of some popular preacher whom a dozen members of the flock desire to entertain, while the less distinguished visitors must bide their time and be stuck in when and where they may. The "big guns" of the Church are all present, and all the "little guns" are scattered about them, popping and snapping every time a "big gun" booms.

But of all the days of commotion and excitement, the climax is ordination day, when candidates for the ministry, college students, and local preachers are examined and either rejected or admitted to the company of the elect. It is common on that day for some old dignitary of the church, seldom a less person than the president of the Conference himself, to preach the sermon. Then, if the fatted calf is not killed, at least the fatted fowls are, and feasting and rejoicing rule the occasion.

This ordination day was no exception. A class of ten stood up before the examining committee and answered the questions put to them. Among them stood Frederick Brent. He wished, he tried, to fail in his answers and be rejected, even though it meant disgrace; but, try as he would, he could not. Force of habit was too strong for him; or was it that some unseen and relentless power was carrying him on and on against his will? He clinched his hands; the beads of perspiration broke out on his brow; but ever as the essential questions came to him his tongue seemed to move of its own volition, without command from the brain, and the murmurs of approval told him that he was answering aright. Never did man struggle harder for brilliant success than this one for ignominious failure. Then some whisper in his consciousness told him that it was over. He felt the laying of hands upon his head. He heard the old minister saying, "Behold, even from the lowliest God taketh His workers," and he felt a flash of resentment, but it was only momentary. He was benumbed. Something seemed to be saying in his mind, "Will the old fool never have done?" But it did not appear to be himself. It was afar off and apart from him. The next he knew, a wet cheek was laid against his own. It was Aunt Hester. She was crying and holding his hand. Afterwards people were shaking hands with him and offering their congratulations; but he answered them in a helpless, mechanical way, as he had answered the questions.

He sat through the sermon and heard it not. But some interest revived in him as the appointments were being read. He heard the president say, "It gives me pain to announce the resignation of one who has so long served in the Master's vineyard, but our dear brother Simpson has decided that he is too old for active work, and has asked to be retired. While we do this with pain and sorrow for the loss—though we do not wholly lose him—of so able a man, we feel that we cannot do better than appoint as his successor in this charge the young man whom you have all seen so brilliantly enter into the ranks of consecrated workers, the Rev. Frederick Brent."

A murmur of approval went round the assembly, and a few open "amens" broke forth as the unctuous old ecclesiastic sat down. It sounded to the ears of the young preacher like the breaking of waves on a far-off shore; and then the meaning of all that had happened sifted through his benumbed intellect, and he strove to rise. He would refuse to act. He would protest. He would tell them that he did not want to preach. But something held him down. He could not rise. The light went blue and green and purple before him. The church, with its sea of faces, spun round and round; his head fell forward.

"He has fainted," said some one.

"The excitement has been too much for him."

"Poor young man, he has been studying too hard, working for this."

They carried him out and took him home, and one of the elders offered a special prayer for his speedy recovery, and that, being recovered, he might bear his new responsibilities with becoming meekness.

When the young minister came to himself, he was lying on the bed in his own room, and Mrs. Hodges, Eliphalet, and a doctor were bending over him.

"He's coming round all right now," said the medical man. "You won't need me any longer." And he departed.

"How are you now, Fred?" asked Mrs. Hodges.

The young man closed his eyes again and did not answer. He had awakened to a full realisation of his position, and a dull misery lay at his heart. He wished that he could die then and there, for death seemed the only escape from his bondage. He was bound, irrevocably bound.

"Poor child," Mrs. Hodges went on, "it was awful tryin' on his nerves. Joy is worse 'n sorrow, sometimes; an' then he'd been workin' so hard. I'd never 'a' believed he could do it, ef Brother Simpson hadn't stuck up fur it."

"She knew it, then," thought Fred. "It was all planned."

"I don't think you'd better talk, Hester," said her husband, in a low voice. He had seen a spasm pass over the face of the prostrate youth.

"Well, I'll go out an' see about the dinner. Some o' the folks I've invited will be comin' in purty soon, an' others'll be droppin' in to inquire how he is. I do hope he'll be well enough to come to the table: it won't seem hardly like an ordination dinner without the principal person. Jes' set by him, 'Liphalet, an' give him them drops the doctor left."

As soon as he heard the door close behind her, Brent opened his eyes and suddenly laid his hand on the old man's shoulder. "You won't let anybody see me, Uncle 'Liph? you won't let them come in here?"

"No, no, my boy, not ef you don't want 'em," said the old man.

"I shall have to think it all over before I see any one. I am not quite clear yet."

"I 'low it was unexpected."

"Did you know, Uncle 'Liph?" he asked, fixing his eyes upon his old friend's face.

"I know'd they was a-plannin' somethin', but I never could find out what, or I would have told you."

A look of relief passed over Brent's face. Just then Mrs. Hodges opened the door. "Here's Elizabeth to see him," she said.

"'Sh," said the old man with great ostentation; and tiptoeing over to the door he partly drew it to, putting his head outside to whisper, "He is too weak; it ain't best fur him to see nobody now."

He closed the door and returned to his seat. "It was 'Lizabeth," he said. "Was I right?"

For answer the patient arose from the bed and walked weakly over to his side.

"Tut, tut, tut, Freddie," said Eliphalet, hesitating over the name. "You'd better lay down now; you ain't any too strong yet."

The young man leaned heavily on his chair, and looked into his friend's eyes: "If God had given me such a man as you as a father, or even as a guardian, I would not have been damned," he said.

"'Sh,'sh, my boy. Don't say that. You're goin' to be all right; you're—you're—" Eliphalet's eyes were moist, and his voice choked here. Rising, he suddenly threw his arms around Fred's neck, crying, "You are my son. God has give you to me to nurse in the time of your trial."

The young man returned the embrace; and so Mrs. Hodges found them when she opened the door softly and peered in. She closed it noiselessly and withdrew.

"Well, I never!" she said. There was a questioning wonder in her face.

"I don't know what to make of them two," she added; "they couldn't have been lovin'er ef they had been father and son."

After a while the guests began to arrive for the dinner. Many were the inquiries and calls for the new minister, but to them all Eliphalet made the same answer: "He ain't well enough to see folks."

Mrs. Hodges herself did her best to bring him out, or to get him to let some of the guests in, but he would not. Finally her patience gave way, and she exclaimed, "Well, now, Frederick Brent, you must know that you air the pastor of a church, an' you've got to make some sacrifices for people's sake. Ef you kin possibly git up,—an' I know you kin,—you ought to come out an' show yoreself for a little while, anyhow. You've got some responsibilities now."

"I didn't ask for them," he answered, coldly. There was a set look about his lips. "Neither will I come out or see any one. If I am old enough to be the pastor of a church, I am old enough to know my will and have it."

Mrs. Hodges was startled at the speech. She felt vaguely that there was a new element in the boy's character since morning. He was on the instant a man. It was as if clay had suddenly hardened in the potter's hands. She could no longer mould or ply him. In that moment she recognised the fact.

The dinner was all that could be expected, and her visitors enjoyed it, in spite of the absence of the guest of honour, but for the hostess it was a dismal failure. After wielding the sceptre for years, it had been suddenly snatched from her hand; and she felt lost and helpless, deprived of her power.

CHAPTER XIII

As Brent thought of the long struggle before him, he began to wish that there might be something organically wrong with him which the shock would irritate into fatal illness. But even while he thought this he sneered at himself for the weakness. A weakness self-confessed holds the possibility of strength. So in a few days he rallied and took up the burden of his life again. As before he had found relief in study, now he stilled his pains and misgivings by a strict attention to the work which his place involved.

His was not an easy position for a young man. He had to go through the ordeal of pastoral visits. He had to condole with old ladies who thought a preacher had nothing else to do than to listen to the recital of their ailments. He had to pray with poor and stricken families whose conditions reminded him strongly of what his own must have been. He had to speak words of serious admonition to girls nearly his own age, who thought it great fun and giggled in his face. All this must he do, nor must he slight a single convention. No rules of conduct are so rigid as are those of a provincial town. He who ministers to the people must learn their prejudices and be adroit enough not to offend them or strong enough to break them down. It was a great load to lay on the shoulders of so young a man. But habit is everything, and he soon fell into the ways of his office. Writing to Taylor, he said, "I am fairly harnessed now, and at work, and, although the pulling is somewhat hard, I know my way. It is wonderful how soon a man falls into the cant of his position and learns to dole out the cut-and-dried phrases of ministerial talk like a sort of spiritual phonograph. I must confess, though, that I am rather good friends with the children who come to my Sunday-school. My own experiences as a child are so fresh in my memory that I rather sympathise with the little fellows, and do all I can to relieve the half-scared stiffness with which they conduct themselves in church and the Sunday-school room.

"I wonder why it is we make church such a place of terror to the young ones. No wonder they quit coming as soon as they can choose.

"I shock Miss Simpson, who teaches a mixed class, terribly, by my freedom with the pupils. She says that she can't do anything with her charges any more; but I notice that her class and the school are growing. I've been at it for several weeks now, and, like a promising baby, I am beginning to take an interest in things.

"If I got on with the old children of my flock as well as I do with the young ones, I should have nothing to complain of; but I don't. They know as little as the youngsters, and are a deal more unruly. They are continually comparing me with their old pastor, and it is needless to say that I suffer by the comparison. The ex-pastor himself burdens me with advice. I shall tell him some day that he has resigned. But I am growing diplomatic, and have several reasons for not wishing to offend him. For all which 'shop' pray forgive me."

One of the reasons for not wishing to offend the Rev. Mr. Simpson of which Brent wrote was, as may be readily inferred, his engagement to Elizabeth. It had not yet officially become public property, but few of Dexter's observant and forecasting people who saw them together doubted for a moment that it would be a match. Indeed, some spiteful people in the community, who looked on from the outside, said that "Mr. Simpson never thought of resigning until he saw that he could keep the place in the family." But of course they were Baptists who said this, or Episcopalians, or Presbyterians,— some such unregenerate lot.

Contrary to the adage, the course of love between the young people did run smooth. The young minister had not disagreed with the older one, so Elizabeth had not disagreed with him, because she did not have to take sides. She was active in the Sunday-school and among the young people's societies, and Brent thought that she would make an ideal minister's wife. Every Sunday, after church, they walked home together, and sometimes he would stop at the house for a meal. They had agreed that at the end of his first pastoral year they would be married; and both parent and guardian smiled on the prospective union.

As his beloved young friend seemed to grow more settled and contented, Eliphalet Hodges waxed more buoyant in the joy of his hale old age, and his wife, all her ambitions satisfied, grew more primly genial every day.

Brent found his congregation increasing, and heard himself

spoken of as a popular preacher. Under these circumstances, it would seem that there was nothing to be desired to make him happy. But he was not so, though he kept an unruffled countenance. He felt the repression that his position put upon him. He prayed that with time it might pass off, but this prayer was not answered. There were times when, within his secret closet, the contemplation of the dead level of his life, as it spread out before him, drove him almost to madness.

The bitterness in his heart against his father had not abated one jot, and whenever these spasms of discontent would seize him he was wont to tell himself, "I am fighting old Tom Brent now, and I must conquer him."

Thus nearly a year passed away, and he was beginning to think of asking Elizabeth to name the day. He had his eye upon a pretty little nest of a house, sufficiently remote from her father's, and he was looking forward to settling quietly down in a home of his own.

It was about this time that, as he sat alone one evening in the little chamber which was his study and bedroom in one, Mr. Simpson entered and opened conversation with him.

For some time a rumour which did violence to the good name of Sophy Davis had been filtering through the community. But it had only filtered, until the girl's disappearance a day or two before had allowed the gossips to talk openly, and great was the talk. The young minister had looked on and listened in silence. He had always known and liked Sophy, and if what the gossips said of her was true, he pitied the girl.

On this particular evening it was plain that Mr. Simpson had come to talk about the affair. After some preliminary remarks, he said, "You have a great chance, dear Brother Brent, for giving the devil in this particular part of the moral vineyard a hard blow."

"I don't clearly see why now, more than before," returned Brent.

"Because you are furnished with a living example of the fruits of evil: don't you see?"

"If there is such an example furnished, the people will see it for themselves, and I should be doing a thankless task to point it out to them. I would rather show people the beauty of good than the ugliness of evil."

"Yes, that's the milk-and-water new style of preaching."

"Well, we all have our opinions, to be sure, but I think it rather a good style." Brent was provokingly nonchalant, and his attitude irritated the elder man.

"We won't discuss that: we will be practical. I came to advise you to hold Sophy Davis up in church next Sunday as a fearful example of evil-doing. You needn't mention any names, but you can make it strong and plain enough."

Brent flushed angrily. "Are there not enough texts in here," he asked, laying his hand upon the Bible, "that I can cite and apply, without holding up a poor weak mortal to the curiosity, scorn, and derision of her equally weak fellows?"

"But it is your duty as a Christian and a preacher of the gospel to use this warning."

"I do not need to kick a falling girl to find examples to warn people from sin; and as for duty, I think that each man best knows his own."

"Then you aren't going to do it?"

"No," the young man burst forth. "I am a preacher of the gospel, not a clerical gossip!"

"Do you mean that I am a gossip?"

"I was not thinking of you."

"Let me preach for you, Sunday."

"I will not do that either. I will not let my pulpit be debased by anything which I consider so low as this business."

"You will not take advice, then?"

"Not such as that."

"Be careful, Frederick Brent. I gave you that pulpit, and I can take it away,—I that know who you are and what you come from."

"The whole town knows what you know, so I do not care for that. As for taking my pulpit from me, you may do that when you please. You put it upon me by force, and by force you may take it; but while I am pastor there I shall use my discretion in all matters of this kind."

"Sophy's been mighty quiet in her devilment. She doesn't accuse anybody. Maybe you've got more than one reason for shielding her."

Brent looked into the man's eyes and read his meaning; then he arose abruptly and opened the door.

"I'm not accusing—"

"Go," said the young man hoarsely. His face was white, and his teeth were hard set.

"You'll learn some respect for your elders yet, if—"

"Go!" Brent repeated, and he took a step towards his visitor. Mr.

90

Simpson looked startled for a moment, but he glanced back into the young man's face and then passed hurriedly out of the room.

Brent let two words slip between his clenched teeth: "The hound!"

No one knew what had passed between the young pastor and Mr. Simpson, but many mutterings and head-shakings of the latter indicated that all was not right. No one knew? Perhaps that is hardly correct, for on Sunday, the sermon over, when Brent looked to find Elizabeth in her usual place whence they walked home together, she was gone. He bit his lip and passed on alone, but it rankled within him that she had so easily believed ill of him.

But he had not seen the last of the Rev. Mr. Simpson's work. It was the right of five members of the congregation to call a church-meeting, and when he returned for service in the evening he found upon the pulpit the written request for such an assembly to be held on Tuesday night. Heading the list of members was the name of the former pastor, although this was not needed to tell the young man that it was his work. In anger he gave out the notice and went on with his duties.

"Somethin' must 'a' riled you to-night, Fred," said Eliphalet when church was out. "You give 'em a mighty stirrin' touch o' fire. It 'minded me o' that old supply sermon." Brent smiled mirthlessly. He knew that the same feelings had inspired both efforts.

On Tuesday evening he was early at church, and in the chair, as was the pastor's place. Early as he was, he did not much precede Mr. Simpson, who came in, followed by a coterie of his choicest spirits.

When the assembly had been duly called to order, Brent asked, "Will some one now please state the object of this meeting?"

Mr. Simpson arose.

"Brothers and sisters," he said, "the object of this meeting is a very simple one. From the time that I began to preach in this church, twenty-five years ago, we had purity and cleanness in the pulpit and in the pew."

Brent's eyes were flashing. Eliphalet Hodges, who had thought that the extra session was for some routine business, pricked up his ears.

Simpson proceeded: "One in this flock has lately gone astray: she has fallen into evil ways—"

"Brother Simpson," interrupted Brent, his face drawn and hard with anger, "will you state the object of this meeting?"

"If the pastor is not afraid to wait, he will see that that is what I am doing."

"Then you are bringing into the church matters that have no business here."

"We shall see about that. We intend to investigate and see why you refused to hold up as a warning one of the sinners of this connection. We propose to ask whom you were shielding—a sinner in the pew, or a sinner in the pulpit as well. We propose—"

"Stop!" The young man's voice broke out like the report of a rifle. "Stop, I say, or, as God sees me, here in His temple, at His very altar, I will do you violence. I speak to you not as your pastor, but as a man: not as an accused man, for you dare not accuse me."

The church was in a commotion. In all its long history, such a scene had never before been enacted within the sacred walls. The men sat speechless; the women shrank far down into their seats. Only those two men, the young and the old, stood glaring into each other's faces.

"Remember, brethren," said someone, recovering himself, "that this is the house of God, and that you are preachers of the gospel."

"I do remember that it is God's house, and for that reason I will not let it be disgraced by scandal that would stain the lowest abode of vice. I do remember that I am a preacher, and for that reason I will not see the gospel made vindictive,—a scourge to whip down a poor girl, who may have sinned,—I know not,—but who, if she did, has an advocate with God. Once before in this place have I told you my opinion of your charity and your love. Once before have I branded you as mockeries of the idea of Christianity. Now I say to you, you are hypocrites. You are like carrion birds who soar high up in the ether for a while and then swoop down to revel in filth and rottenness. The stench of death is sweet to you. Putridity is dear to you. As for you who have done this work, you need pity. Your own soul must be reeking with secret foulness to be so basely suspicious. Your own eyes must have cast unholy glances to so soon accuse the eyes of others. As for the thing which you, mine enemy, have intimated here to-night, as pastor of this church I scorn to make defence. But as a man I say, give such words as those breath again, and I will forget your age and only remember your infamy. I see the heads of some about me here wagging, some that knew my father. I hear their muffled whispers, and I know what they are saying. I know what is in their hearts. You are saying that it is the old Tom

Brent in me showing itself at last. Yes, it has smouldered in me long, and I am glad. I think better of that spirit because it was waked into life to resent meanness. I would rather be the most roistering drunkard that ever reeled down these streets than call myself a Christian and carouse over the dead characters of my fellows.

"To-night I feel for the first time that I am myself. I give you back gladly what you have given me. I am no longer your pastor. We are well quit. Even while I have preached to you, I have seen in your hearts your scorn and your distrust, and I have hated you in secret. But I throw off the cloak. I remove the disguise. Here I stand stripped of everything save the fact that I am a man; and I despise you openly. Yes, old Tom, drunken Tom Brent's son despises you. Go home. Go home. There may be work for your stench-loving nostrils there."

He stood like an avenging spirit, pointing towards the door, and the people who had sat there breathless through it all rose quietly and slipped out. Simpson joined them and melted into the crowd. They were awed and hushed.

Only Mrs. Hodges, white as death, and her husband, bowed with grief, remained. A silent party, they walked home together. Not until they were in the house did the woman break down, and then she burst into a storm of passionate weeping as if the pent-up tears of all her stoical life were flowing at once.

"Oh, Fred, Fred," she cried between her sobs, "I see it all now. I was wrong. I was wrong. But I did it all fur the best. The Lord knows I did it fur the best."

"I know you did, Aunt Hester, but I wish you could have seen sooner, before the bitterness of death had come into my life." He felt strangely hard and cold. Her grief did not affect him then.

"Don't take on so, Hester," said the old man, but the woman continued to rock herself to and fro and moan, "I did it fur the best, I did it fur the best." The old man took her in his arms, and after a while she grew more calm, only her sobs breaking the silence.

"I shall go away to-morrow," said Brent. "I am going out into the world for myself. I've been a disgrace to every one connected with me."

"Don't say that about yoreself, Fred; I ain't a-goin' to hear it," said Eliphalet. "You've jest acted as any right-thinkin' man would 'a' acted. It wouldn't 'a' been right fur you to 'a' struck Brother Simpson, but I'm nearer his age, an' my hands itched to git a hold o' him." The old man looked menacing, and his fist involuntarily clenched.

"'Liphalet," said his wife, "I've been a-meddlin' with the business o' Providence, an' I've got my jest desserts. I thought I knowed jest what He wanted me to do, an' I was more ignorant than a child. Furgive me ef you kin, Fred, my boy. I was tryin' to make a good man o' you."

"There's nothing for me to forgive, Aunt Hester. I'm sorry I've spoiled your plans."

"I'm glad, fur mebbe God'll have a chance now to work His own plans. But pore little 'Lizabeth!"

Brent's heart hurt him as he heard the familiar name, and he turned abruptly and went to his room. Once there, he had it out with himself. "But," he told himself, "if I had the emergency to meet again, I should do the same thing."

The next morning's mail brought him a little packet in which lay the ring he had given Elizabeth to plight their troth.

"I thank you for this," he said. "It makes my way easier."

CHAPTER XIV

The story of the altercation between the young minister and a part of his congregation was well bruited about the town, and all united in placing the fault heavily on the young man's shoulders. As for him, he did not care. He was wild with the enjoyment of his new-found freedom. Only now and again, as he sat at the table the morning after, and looked into the sad faces of Eliphalet and his guardian, did he feel any sorrow at the turn matters had taken.

In regard to Elizabeth, he felt only relief. It was as if a half-defined idea in his mind had been suddenly realised. For some time he had believed her unable either to understand him or to sympathise with his motives. He had begun to doubt the depth of his own feeling for her. Then had come her treatment of him last Sunday, and somehow, while he knew it was at her father's behest, he could not help despising her weakness.

He had spent much of the night before in packing his few effects, and all was now ready for his departure as they sat at breakfast. Mrs. Hodges was unusually silent, and her haggard face and swollen eyes told how she had passed the night. All in a single hour she had seen the work of the best part of her life made as naught, and she was bowed with grief and defeat. Frederick Brent's career had really been her dream. She had scarcely admitted, even to herself, how deeply his success affected her own happiness. She cared for him in much the same way that a sculptor loves his statue. Her attitude was that of one who says, "Look upon this work; is it not fair? I made it myself." It was as much her pride as it was her love that was hurt, because her love had been created by her pride. She had been prepared to say, exultingly, "Look where he came from, and look where he is;" and now his defection deprived her for ever of that sweet privilege. People had questioned her ability to train up a boy rightly, and she had wished to refute their imputations, by making that boy the wonder of the community and their spiritual leader; and just as she had deemed her work safely done, lo, it had come toppling about her ears. Even if the fall had come sooner, she would have felt it less. It was the more terrible because so unexpected, for she had laid aside all her fears and misgivings and felt secure in her achievement.

"You ain't a-eatin' nothin', Hester," said her husband, anxiously. "I hope you ain't a-feelin' bad this mornin'." He had heard her sobbing all night long, and the strength and endurance of her grief frightened him and made him uneasy, for she had always been so stoical. "Hadn't you better try an' eat one o' them buckwheat cakes? Put lots o' butter an' molasses on it; they're mighty good."

"Ef they're so good, why don't you eat yoreself? You been foolin' with a half a one for the last ten minutes." Indeed, the old man's food did seem to stick in his throat, and once in a while a mist would come up before his eyes. He too had had his dreams, and one of them was of many a happy evening spent with his beloved boy, who should be near him, a joy and comfort in the evening of his life; and now he was going away.

The old man took a deep gulp at his coffee to hide his emotion. It burned his mouth and gave reason for the moisture in his eye when he looked up at Fred.

"What train air you goin' to take, Fred?" he asked.

"I think I'll catch that eight-fifty flier. It's the best I can get, you know, and vestibuled through, too."

"You have jest finally made up yore mind to go, have you?"

"Nothing could turn me from it now, Uncle 'Liph."

"It seems like a shame. You 'ain't got nothin' to do down in Cincinnaty."

"I'll find something before long. I am going to spend the first few days just in getting used to being free." The next moment he was sorry that he had said it, for he saw his guardian's eyes fill.

"I am sorry, Frederick," she said, with some return to her old asperity, "I am sorry that I've made your life so hard that you think that you have been a slave. I am sorry that my home has been so onpleasant that you're so powerful glad to git away from it, even to go into a strange city full of wickedness an' sin."

"I didn't mean it that way, Aunt Hester. You've been as good as you could be to me. You have done your duty by me, if any one ever could."

"Well, I am mighty glad you realise that, so's ef you go away an' fall into sinful ways you can't lay none of it to my bringin'-up."

"I feel somehow as if I would like to have a go with sin some time, to see what it is like."

"Well, I lay you'll be satisfied before you've been in Cincinnaty long, for ef there ever was livin' hells on airth, it's them big cities."

"Oh, I have got faith to believe that Fred ain't a-goin' to do nothin' wrong," said Eliphalet.

"Nobody don't know what nobody's a-goin' to do under temptation sich as is layin' in wait fur young men in the city, but I'm shore I've done my best to train you right, even ef I have made some mistakes in my poor weak way an' manner."

"If I do fall into sinful ways, Aunt Hester, I shall never blame you or your training for it."

"But you ain't a-goin' to do it, Fred; you ain't a-goin' to fall into no evil ways."

"I don't know, Uncle 'Liph. I never felt my weakness more than I do now."

"Then that very feelin' will be yore stren'th, my boy. Keep on feelin' that way."

"It'll not be a stren'th in Cincinnaty, not by no means. There is too many snares an' pitfalls there to entrap the weak," Mrs. Hodges insisted.

It is one of the defects of the provincial mind that it can never see any good in a great city. It concludes that, as many people are wicked, where large numbers of human beings are gathered together there must be a much greater amount of evil than in a smaller place. It overlooks the equally obvious reasoning that, as some people are good, in the larger mass there must be also a larger amount of goodness. It seems a source of complacent satisfaction to many to sit in contemplation of the fact of the extreme wickedness of the world. They are like children who delight in a "bluggy" story,—who gloat over murder and rapine.

Brent, however, was in no wise daunted by the picture of evil which his guardian painted for him, and as soon as breakfast was over he got his things in hand ready to start. Buoyant as he was with his new freedom, this was a hard moment for him. Despite the severity of his youthful treatment in Dexter, the place held all the tender recollections he had, and the room where he stood was the scene of some memories that now flooded his mind and choked his utterance when he strove to say good-bye. He had thought that he should do it with such a fine grace. He would prove such a strong man. But he found his eyes suffused with tears, as he held his old guardian's hand, for, in spite of all, she had done the best for him that she knew, and she had taken a hard, uncompromising pride in him.

"I hope you'll git along all right, Frederick," she faltered forth tearfully. "Keep out of bad company, an' let us hear from you whenever you can. The Lord knows I've tried to do my dooty by you."

Poor Eliphalet tried to say something as he shook the young man's hand, but he broke down and wept like a child. The boy could not realise what a deal of sunshine he was taking out of the old man's life.

"I'll write to you as soon as I am settled," he told them, and with a husky farewell hurried away from the painful scene. At the gate the old couple stood and watched him go swinging down the street towards the station. Then they went into the house, and sat long in silence in the room he had so lately left. The breakfast-table, with all that was on it, was left standing unnoticed and neglected, a thing unprecedented in Mrs. Hodges' orderly household.

Finally her husband broke the silence. "It 'pears as if we had jest buried some one and come home from the funeral."

"An' that's jest what we have done, ef we only knowed it, 'Liphalet. We've buried the last of the Fred Brent we knowed an' raised. Even ef we ever see him ag'in, he'll never be the same to us. He'll have new friends to think of an' new notions in his head."

"Don't say that, Hester; don't say that. I can't stand it. He is never goin' to furgit you an' me, an' it hurts me to hear you talk like that."

"It don't soun' none too pleasant fur me, 'Liphalet, but I've learned to face the truth, an' that's the truth ef it ever was told."

"Well, mebbe it's fur the best, then. It'll draw us closer together and make us more to each other as we journey down to the end. It's our evenin', Hester, an' we must expect some chilly winds 'long towards night, but I guess He knows best." He reached over and took his wife's hand tenderly in his, and so they sat on sadly, but gathering peace in the silence and the sympathy, until far into the morning.

Meanwhile the eight-fifty "flier" was speeding through the beautiful Ohio Valley, bearing the young minister away from the town of his birth. Out of sight of the grief of his friends, he had regained all his usual stolid self-possession, though his mind often went back to the little cottage at Dexter where the two old people sat, and he may be forgiven if his memory lingered longer over the image of the man than of the woman. He remembered with a thrill at his heart what Eliphalet Hodges had been to him in the dark days of his youth, and he confessed to himself with a half shame that his greatest regret was in leaving him.

The feeling with which he had bidden his guardian good-bye was one not of regret at his own loss, but of pity for her distress. To Elizabeth his mind only turned for a moment to dismiss her with a mild contempt. Something hard that had always been in his nature seemed to have suddenly manifested itself.

"It is so much better this way," he said, "for if the awakening had come later we should have been miserable together." And then his thoughts went forward to the new scenes towards which he was speeding.

He had never been to Cincinnati. Indeed, except on picnic days, he had scarcely ever been outside of Dexter. But Cincinnati was the great city of his State, the one towards which adventurous youth turned its steps when real life was to be begun. He dreaded and yet longed to be there, and his heart was in a turmoil of conflicting emotion as he watched the landscape flit by.

It was a clear August day. Nature was trembling and fainting in the ecstasies of sensuous heat. Beside the railway the trenches which in spring were gurgling brooks were now dry and brown, and the reeds which had bent forward to kiss the water now leaned over from very weakness, dusty and sickly. The fields were ripening to the harvest. There was in the air the smell of fresh-cut hay. The corn-stalks stood like a host armed with brazen swords to resist the onslaught of that other force whose weapon was the corn-knife. Farther on, between the trees, the much depleted river sparkled in the sun and wound its way, now near, now away from the road, a glittering dragon in an enchanted wood.

Such scenes as these occupied the young man's mind, until, amid the shouts of brake-men, the vociferous solicitations of the baggage-man, and a general air of bustle and preparation, the train thundered into the Grand Central Station. Something seized Brent's heart like a great compressing hand. He was frightened for an instant, and then he was whirled out with the rest of the crowd, up the platform, through the thronged waiting-room, into the street.

Then the cries of the eager men outside of "Cab, sir? cab, sir?" "Let me take your baggage," and "Which way, sir?" bewildered him. He did the thing which every provincial does: he went to a policeman and inquired of him where he might find a respectable boarding-house. The policeman did not know, but informed him that there were plenty of hotels farther up. With something like disgust, Brent wondered if all the hotels were like those he saw at the station, where the guests had to go through the bar-room to reach their chambers. He shuddered at it; so strong is the influence of habit. But he did not wish to go to a hotel: so, carrying his two valises, he trudged on, though the hot sun of the mid-afternoon beat mercilessly down upon him. He kept looking into the faces of people who passed him, in the hope that he might see in one encouragement to ask for the information he so much wanted; but one and all they hurried by without even so much as a glance at the dusty traveller. Had one of them looked at him, he would merely have said, mentally, "Some country bumpkin come in to see the sights of town and be buncoed."

There is no loneliness like the loneliness of the unknown man in a crowd. A feeling of desolation took hold upon Brent, so he turned down a side-street in order to be more out of the main line of business. It was a fairly respectable quarter; children were playing about the pavements and in the gutters, while others with pails and pitchers were going to and from the corner saloon, where their vessels were filled with foaming beer. Brent wondered at the cruelty of parents who thus put their children in the way of temptation, and looked to see if the little ones were not bowed with shame; but they all strode stolidly on, with what he deemed an unaccountable indifference to their own degradation. He passed one place where the people were drinking in the front yard, and saw a mother holding a glass of beer to her little one's lips. He could now understand the attitude of the children, but the fact, nevertheless, surprised and sickened him.

Finally, the sign "Boarding Here" caught his eye. He went into the yard and knocked at the door. A plump German girl opened it, and, to his question as to accommodation, replied that she would see her mistress. He was ushered into a little parlour that boasted some shabby attempts at finery, and was soon joined by a woman whom he took to be the "lady of the house."

Yes, Mrs. Jones took boarders. Would he want room and board?

Terms five dollars per week. Had he work in the city? No? Well, from gentlemen who were out of work she always had her money in advance. But would he see his room first?

Wondering much at Mrs. Jones's strange business arrangement, Brent allowed her to conduct him to a room on the second floor, which looked out on the noisy street. It was not a palatial place by any means, but was not uncomfortable save for the heat, which might be expected anywhere on such a day. He was tired and wanted rest, so he engaged the place and paid the woman then and there.

"You just come off the train, I see. Will you have luncheon at once, Mr.—?"

"Brent," said he. "Yes, I will have some luncheon, if you please."

"Do you take beer with your luncheon?"

"No-o," he said, hesitating; and yet why should he not take beer? Everybody else did, even the children. Then he blushed as he thought of what his aunt Hester would think of his even hesitating over the question. She would have shot out a "no" as if it were an insult to be asked. So without beer he ate his luncheon and lay down to rest for the afternoon. When one has travelled little, even a short journey is fatiguing.

In the evening Brent met some of the other boarders at supper; there were not many. They were principally clerks in shops or under-bookkeepers. One genial young fellow struck up a conversation with Fred, and became quite friendly during the evening.

"I guess you will go out to the 'Zoo' to-morrow, won't you? That is about the first place that visitors usually strike for when they come here."

"I thought of getting a general idea of the city first, so that I could go round better before going farther out."

"Oh, you won't have any trouble in getting around. Just ask folks, and they will direct you anywhere."

"But everybody seems to be in a hurry; and by the time I open my mouth to ask them, they have passed me."

The young clerk, Mr. Perkins by name, thought this was a great joke and laughed long and loudly at it.

"I wish to gracious I could go around with you. I have been so busy ever since I have been here that I have never seen any of the show sights myself. But I tell you what I will do: I can steer you around some on Thursday night. That is my night off, and then I will show you some sights that are sights." The young man chuckled as he got his hat and prepared to return to the shop. Brent thanked him in a way that sounded heavy and stilted even to his own ears after the other's light pleasantry.

"And another thing," said Perkins, "we will go to see the base-ball game on Sunday, Clevelands and the Reds,—great game, you know." It was well that Mr. Perkins was half-way out of the door before he finished his sentence, for there was no telling what effect upon him the flush which mounted to Brent's face and the horror in his eyes would have had.

Go to a baseball game on Sunday! What would his people think of such a thing? How would he himself feel there,—he, notwith-standing his renunciation of office, a minister of the gospel? He hastened to his room, where he could be alone and think. The city indeed was full of temptations to the young! And yet he knew he would be ashamed to tell his convictions to Perkins, or to explain his horror at the proposition. Again there came to him, as there had come many times before, the realisation that he was out of accord with his fellows. He was not in step with the procession. He had been warped away from the parallel of every-day, ordinary humanity. In order to still the tumult in his breast, he took his hat and wandered out upon the street. He wanted to see people, to come into contact with them and so rub off some of the strangeness in which their characters appeared to him.

The streets were all alight and alive with bustle. Here a fakir with loud voice and market-place eloquence was vending his shoddy wares; there a drunkard reeled or was kicked from the door of a saloon, whose noiselessly swinging portals closed for an instant only to be reopened to admit another victim, who ere long would be treated likewise. A quartet of young negroes were singing on the pavement in front of a house as he passed and catching the few pennies and nickels that were flung to them from the door. A young girl smiled and beckoned to him from a window, and another who passed laughed saucily up into his face and cried, "Ah, there!" Everywhere was the inevitable pail flashing to and fro. Sickened, disgusted, thrown back upon himself, Brent turned his steps homeward again. Was this the humanity he wanted to know? Was this the evil which he wanted to have a go with? Was Aunt Hester, after all, in the right, and was her way the best? His heart was torn by a multitude of conflicting emotions. He had wondered, in one of his rebellious moods, if, when he was perfectly untrammelled, he would ever pray; but on this night of nights, before he went wearily to bed, he remained long upon his knees.

CHAPTER XV

Brent found himself in a most peculiar situation. He had hated the severe discipline of his youth, and had finally rebelled against it and renounced its results as far as they went materially. This he had thought to mean his emancipation. But when the hour to assert his freedom had come, he found that the long years of rigid training had bound his volition with iron bands. He was wrapped in a mantle of habit which he was ashamed to display and yet could not shake off. The pendulum never stops its swing in the middle of the arc. So he would have gone to the other extreme and revelled in the pleasures whose very breath had been forbidden to his youth; but he found his sensibilities revolting from everything that did not accord with the old Puritan code by which they had been trained. He knew himself to be full of capabilities for evil, but it seemed as if some power greater than his held him back. It was Frederick Brent who looked on sin abstractly, but its presence in the concrete was seen through the eyes of Mrs. Hester Hodges. It could hardly be called the decree of conscience, because so instantaneous was the rejection of evil that there was really no time for reference to the internal monitor. The very restriction which he had complained of he was now putting upon himself. The very yoke whose burden he hated he was placing about his own neck. He had run away from the sound of "right" and "duty," but had not escaped their power. He felt galled, humiliated, and angry with himself, because he had long seen the futility of blind indignation against the unseen force which impelled him forward in a hated path.

One thing that distressed him was a haunting fear of the sights which Perkins would show him on the morrow's night. He had seen enough for himself to conjecture of what nature they would be. He did not want to see more, and yet how could he avoid it? He might plead illness, but that would be a lie; and then there would be other nights to follow, so it would only be a postponement of what must ultimately take place or be boldly rejected. Once he decided to explain his feelings on the subject, but in his mind's eye he saw the half-pitying sneer on the face of the worldly young cityite, and he quailed before it.

Why not go? Could what he saw hurt him? Was he so great a coward that he dared not come into the way of temptation? We do not know the strength of a shield until it has been tried in battle. Metal does not ring true or false until it is struck. He would go. He would see with his own eyes for the purpose of information. He would have his boasted bout with sin. After this highly valorous conclusion he fell asleep.

The next morning found him wavering again, but he put all his troubled thoughts away and spent the day in sight-seeing. He came in at night tired and feeling strange and lonesome. "Whom the gods wish to destroy, they first make mad," we used to say; but all that is changed now, and whom the devil wishes to get, he first makes lonesome. Then the victim is up to anything.

Brent had finished his supper when Perkins came in, but he brightened at the young clerk's cheery salute, "Hello, there! ready to go, are you?"

"Been ready all day," he replied, with a laugh. "It's been pretty slow."

"'Ain't made much out, then, seeing the sights of this little village of ours? Well, we'll do better to-night, if the people don't see that black tie of yours and take you for a preacher getting facts for a crusade."

Brent blushed and bit his lip, but he only said, "I'll go up and change it while you're finishing your supper."

"Guess you'd better, or some one will be asking you for a sermon." Perkins laughed good-naturedly, but he did not know how his words went home to his companion's sensitive feelings. He thought that his haste in leaving the room and his evident confusion were only the evidence of a greenhorn's embarrassment under raillery. He really had no idea that his comrade's tie was the badge of his despised calling.

Brent was down again in a few minutes, a grey cravat having superseded the offending black. But even now, as he compared himself with his guide, he appeared sombre and ascetic. His black Prince Albert coat showed up gloomy and oppressive against young Perkins's natty drab cutaway relieved by a dashing red tie. From head to foot the little clerk was light and dapper; and as they moved along the crowded streets the preacher felt much as a conscious omnibus would feel beside a pneumatic-tired sulky.

"You can talk all you want to about your Chicago," Perkins was rattling on, "but you can bet your life Cincinnati's the greatest town in the West. Chicago's nothing but a big overgrown country town. Everything looks new and flimsy there to a fellow, but here you get something that's solid. Chicago's pretty swift, too, but there ain't no flies on us, either, when it comes to the go."

Brent thought with dismay how much his companion knew, and felt a passing bitterness that he, though older, had seen none of these things.

"Ever been in Chicago?" asked Perkins; "but of course you haven't." This was uttered in such a tone of conviction that the minister thought his greenness must be very apparent.

"I've never been around much of anywhere," he said. "I've been hard at work all my life."

"Eh, that so? You don't look like you'd done much hard work. What do you do?"

"I—I—ah—write," was the confused answer.

Perkins, fortunately, did not notice the confusion. "Oh, ho!" he said: "do you go in for newspaper work?"

"No, not for newspapers."

"Oh, you're an author, a regular out-and-outer. Well, don't you know, I thought you were somehow different from most fellows I've met. I never could see how you authors could stay away in small towns, where you hardly ever see any one, and write about people as you do; but I suppose you get your people from books."

"No, not entirely," replied Brent, letting the mistake go. "There are plenty of interesting characters in a small town. Its life is just what the life of a larger city is, only the scale is smaller."

"Well, if you're on a search for characters, you'll see some to-night that'll be worth putting in your note-book. We'll stop here first."

The place before which they had stopped was surrounded by a high vine-covered lattice fence: over the entrance flamed forth in letters set with gas-lights the words "Meyer's Beer-Garden and Variety Hall. Welcome." He could hear the sound of music within,—a miserable orchestra, and a woman singing in a high strident voice. People were passing in and out of the place. He hesitated, and then, shaking himself, as if to shake off his scruples, turned towards the entrance. As he reached the door, a man who was standing beside it thrust a paper into his hand. He saw others refuse to take it as they passed. It was only the announcement of a temperance meeting at a neighbouring hall. He raised his eyes to find the gaze of the man riveted upon him.

"Don't you go in there, young man," he said. "You don't look like you was used to this life. Come away. Remember, it's the first step—"

"Chuck him," said Perkins's voice at his elbow. But something in the man's face held him. A happy thought struck him. He turned to his companion and said, in a low voice, "I think I've found a character here already. Will you excuse me for a while?"

"Certainly. Business before pleasure. Pump him all you can, and then come in. You'll find me at one of the tables on the farther side." Perkins passed on.

"You won't go in, my young friend?" said the temperance man.

"What is it to you whether I go in or stay out?" asked Brent, in a tone of assumed carelessness.

"I want to keep every man I kin from walkin' the path that I walked and sufferin' as I suffer." He was seized with a fit of coughing. His face was old and very thin, and his hands, even in that hot air, were blue as with cold. "I wisht you'd go to our meetin' to-night. We've got a powerful speaker there, that'll show you the evils of drink better 'n I kin."

"Where is this great meeting?" Brent tried to put a sneer into his voice, but an unaccountable tremor ruined its effect.

He was duly directed to the hall. "I may come around," he said, carelessly, and sauntered off, leaving the man coughing beside the door of the beer-garden. "Given all of his life to the devil," he mused, "drunk himself to death, and now seeking to steal into heaven by giving away a few tracts in his last worthless moments." He had forgotten all about Perkins.

He strolled about for a while, and then, actuated by curiosity, sought out the hall where the meeting was being held. It was a rude place, in a poor neighbourhood. The meeting-room was up two flights of dingy, rickety stairs. Hither Brent found his way. His acquaintance of the street was there before him and sitting far to the front among those whom, by their position, the young man took to be the speakers of the evening. The room was half full of the motleyest crew that it had ever been his ill fortune to set eyes on.

The flaring light of two lard-oil torches brought out the peculiarities of the queer crowd in fantastic prominence. There was everywhere an odour of work, but it did not hang chiefly about the men. The women were mostly little weazen-faced creatures, whom labour and ill treatment had rendered inexpressibly hideous. The men were chiefly of the reformed. The bleared eyes and bloated faces of some showed that their reformation must have been of very recent occurrence, while a certain unsteadiness in the conduct of others showed that with them the process had not taken place at all.

It was late, and a stuffy little man with a wheezy voice and a very red nose was holding forth on the evils of intemperance, very much to his own satisfaction evidently, and unmistakably to the weariness of his audience. Brent was glad when he sat down. Then there followed experiences from women whose husbands had been drunkards and from husbands whose wives had been similarly afflicted. It was all thoroughly uninteresting and commonplace.

The young man had closed his eyes, and, suppressing a yawn, had just determined to go home, when he was roused by a new stir in the meeting, and the voice of the wheezy man saying "And now, brothers, we are to have a great treat: we are to hear the story of the California Pilgrim, told by himself. Bless the Lord for his testimony! Go on, my brother." Brent opened his eyes and took in the scene. Beside the chairman stood the emaciated form of his chance acquaintance. It was the man's face, now seen in the clearer light, that struck him. It was thin, very thin, and of a deathly pallor. The long grey hair fell in a tumbled mass above the large hollow eyes. The cheek-bones stood up prominently, and seemed almost bursting through the skin. His whole countenance was full of the terrible, hopeless tragedy of a ruined life. He began to speak.

"I'll have to be very brief, brothers and sisters, as I haven't much breath to spare. But I will tell you my life simply, in order to warn any that may be in the same way to change their course. Twenty years ago I was a hard-workin' man in this State. I got along fairly, an' had enough to live on an' keep my wife an' baby decent. Of course I took my dram like the other workmen, an' it never hurt me. But some men can't stand what others kin, an' the habit commenced to grow on me. I took a spree, now an' then, an' then went back to work, fur I was a good hand, an' could always git somethin' to do. After a while I got so unsteady that nobody would have me. From then on it was the old story. I got discouraged, an' drunk all the more. Three years after I begun, my home was a wreck, an' I had ill-treated my wife until she was no better than I was; then she got a divorce from me, an' I left the town. I wandered from place to place, sometimes workin', always drinkin'; sometimes ridin' on trains, sometimes trampin' by the roadside. Fin'lly I drifted out to Californy, an' there I spent most o' my time until, a year ago, I come to see myself what a miserable bein' I was. It was through one of your Bands of Hope. From then I pulled myself up; but it was too late. I had ruined my health. I started for my old home, talkin' and tellin' my story by the way. I want to get back there an' jest let the people know that I've repented, an' then I can die in peace. I want to see ef my wife an' child—" Here a great fit of coughing seized him again, and he was forced to sit down.

Brent had listened breathlessly to every word: a terrible fear was clutching at his heart. When the man sat down, he heard the voice of the chairman saying, "Now let us all contribute what we can to help the brother on his journey; he hasn't far to go. Come forward and lay your contributions on the table here, now. Some one sing. Now who's going to help Brother Brent?"

The young man heard the name. He grasped the seat in front of him for support. He seized his hat, staggered to his feet, and stumbled blindly out of the room and down the stairs.

"Drunk" said some one as he passed.

He rushed into the street, crying within himself, "My God! my God!" He hurried through the crowds, thrusting the people right and left and unheeding the curses that followed him. He reached home and groped up to his room.

"Awful!" murmured Mrs. Jones. "He seemed such a good young man; but he's been out with Mr. Perkins, and men will be men."

Once in his room, it seemed that he would go mad. Back and forth he paced the floor, clenching his hands and smiting his head. He wanted to cry out. He felt the impulse to beat his head against the wall. "My God! my God! It was my father," he cried, "going back home. What shall I do?" There was yet no pity in his heart for the man whom he now knew to be his parent. His only thought was of the bitterness that parent's folly had caused. "Oh, why could he not have died away from home, without going back there to revive all the old memories? Why must he go back there just at this troublous time to distress those who have loved me and help those who hate me to drag my name in the dust? He has chosen his own way, and it has ever been apart from me. He has neglected and forgotten me. Now why does he seek me out, after a life spent among strangers? I do not want him. I will not see him again. I shall never go home. I have seen him, I have heard him talk. I have stood near him and talked with him, and just when I am leaving it all behind me, all my past of sorrow and degradation, he comes and lays a hand upon me, and I am more the son of Tom Brent to-night than ever before. Is it Fate, God, or the devil that pursues me so?"

His passion was spending itself. When he was more calm he thought, "He will go home with a religious testimony on his lips, he will die happy, and the man who has spent all his days in drunkenness, killed his wife, and damned his son will be preached through the gates of glory on the strength of a few words of familiar cant." There came into his mind a great contempt for the system which taught or preached so absurd and unfair a doctrine. "I wish I could go to the other side of the world," he said, "and live among heathens who know no such dreams. I, Frederick Brent, son of Tom Brent, temperance advocate, sometime drunkard and wife-beater." There was terrible, scorching irony in the thought. There was a pitiless hatred in his heart for his father's very name.

"I suppose," he went on, "that Uncle 'Liph"—he said the name tenderly—"has my letter now and will be writing to me to come home and hear my father's dying words, and receive perhaps his dying blessing,—his dying blessing! But I will not go; I will not go back." Anger, mingled with shame at his origin and a greater shame at himself, flamed within him. "He did not care for the helpless son sixteen years ago: let him die without the sight of the son now. His life has cursed my life, his name has blasted my name, his blood has polluted my blood. Let him die as he lived—without me."

He dropped into a chair and struck the table with his clenched fists.

Mrs. Jones came to the door to ask him not to make so much noise. He buried his face in his hands, and sat there thinking, thinking, until morning.

CHAPTER XVI

Next morning when Brent went down to breakfast he was as a man who had passed through an illness. His eyes were bloodshot, his face was pale, his step was nervous and weak.

"Just what I expected," muttered Mrs. Jones. "He was in a beastly condition last night. I shall speak to Mr. Perkins about it. He had no right to take and get him in such a state."

She was more incensed than ever when the gay young clerk came in looking perfectly fresh. "He's used to it," she told herself, "and it doesn't tell on him, but it's nearly killed that poor young man."

"Hullo there, Brent," said Perkins. "You chucked me for good last night. Did you lose your way, or was your 'character' too interesting?"

"Character too interesting," was the laconic reply.

"And I'll bet you've been awake all night studying it out."

"You are entirely right there," said Brent, smiling bitterly. "I haven't slept a wink all night: I've been studying out that character."

"I thought you looked like it. You ought to take some rest today."

"I can't. I've got to put in my time on the same subject."

Mrs. Jones pursed her lips and bustled among the teacups. The idea of their laughing over their escapades right before her face and thinking that she did not understand! She made the mental observation that all men were natural born liars, and most guilty when they appeared to be most innocent. "Character," indeed! Did they think to blind her to the true situation of things? Oh, astute woman!

"Strange fellow," said Perkins to his spoon, when, after a slight breakfast, Brent had left the table.

"There's others that are just as strange, only they think they're sharper," quoth Mrs. Jones, with a knowing look.

"I don't understand you," returned her boarder, turning his attention from his spoon to the lady's face.

"There's none so blind as those who don't want to see."

"Again I say, I don't understand you, Mrs. Jones."

"Oh, Mr. Perkins, it's no use trying to fool me. I know men. In my younger days I was married to a man."

"Strange contingency! But still it casts no light on your previous remarks."

"You've got very innocent eyes, I must say, Mr. Perkins."

"The eyes, madam, are the windows of the soul," Perkins quoted, with mock gravity.

"Well, if the eyes are the soul's windows, there are some people who always keep their windows curtained."

"But I must deny any such questionable performance on my part. I have not the shrewdness to veil my soul from the scrutiny of so keen an observer as yourself."

"Oh, flattery isn't going to do your cause one mite of good, Mr. Perkins. I'm not going to scold, but next time you get him in such a state I wish you'd bring him home yourself, and not let him come tearing in here like a madman, scaring a body half to death."

"Will you kindly explain yourself? What condition? And who is 'him'?"

"Oh, of course you don't know."

"I do not."

"Do you mean to tell me that you weren't out with Mr. Brent last night before he came home?"

"I assuredly was not with him after the first quarter of an hour."

"Well, it's hard to believe that he got that way by himself."

"That way! Why, he left me at the door of Meyer's beer-garden to talk to a temperance crank who he thought was a character."

"Well, no temperance character sent him rushing and stumbling in here as he did last night. 'Character,' indeed! It was at the bottom of a pail of beer or something worse."

"Oh, I don't think he was 'loaded.' He's an author, and I guess his eye got to rolling in a fine frenzy, and he had to hurry home to keep it from rolling out of his head into the street."

"Mr. Perkins, this is no subject for fun. I have seen what I have seen, and it was a most disgraceful spectacle. I take your word for it that you were not with Mr. Brent, but you need not try to go further and defend him."

"I'm not trying to defend him at all; it's really none of my business." And Perkins went off to work, a little bit angry and a good deal more bewildered. "I thought he was a 'jay,'" he remarked.

To Brent the day was a miserable one. He did not leave his room, but spent the slow hours pacing back and forth in absorbed thought, interrupted now and then by vain attempts to read. His mind was in a state of despairing apprehension. It needed no prophetic sense to tell him what would happen. It was only a question of how long a time would elapse before he might expect to receive word from Dexter summoning him home. It all depended upon whether or not the "California Pilgrim" got money enough last night for exploiting his disgraceful history to finish the last stage of the journey.

What disgusted the young man so intensely was that his father, after having led the life he had, should make capital out of relating it. Would not a quiet repentance, if it were real, have been quite sufficient? He very much distrusted the sincerity of motive that made a man hold himself up as an example of reformed depravity, when the hope of gain was behind it all. The very charity which he had preached so fiercely to his congregation he could not extend to his own father. Indeed, it appeared to him (although this may have been a trick of his distorted imagination) that the "Pilgrim" had seemed to take a sort of pleasure in the record of his past, as though it were excellent to be bad, in order to have the pleasure of conversion. His lip involuntarily curled when he thought of conversion. He was disgusted with all men and principles. One man offends, and a whole system suffers. He felt a peculiar self-consciousness, a self-glorification in his own misery. Placing the accumulated morality of his own life against the full-grown evil of his father's, it angered him to think that by the intervention of a seemingly slight quantity the results were made equal.

"What is the use of it all," he asked himself, "my struggle, involuntary though it was, my self-abnegation, my rigidity, when what little character I have built up is overshadowed by my father's past? Why should I have worked so hard and long for those rewards, real or fancied, the favour of God and the respect of men, when he, after a career of outrageous dissipation, by a simple act or claim of repentance wins the Deity's smile and is received into the arms of people with gushing favour, while I am looked upon as the natural recipient of all his evil? Of course they tell us that there is more joy over the one lamb that is found than over the ninety and nine that went not astray; it puts rather a high premium on straying." He laughed bitterly. "With what I have behind me, is it worth being decent for the sake of decency? After all, is the game worth the candle?"

He took up a little book which many times that morning he had been attempting to read. It was an edition of Matthew Arnold's poems, and one of the stanzas was marked. It was in "Mycerinus."

> *Oh, wherefore cheat our youth, if thus it be,*
> *Of one short joy, one lust, one pleasant dream,*
> *Stringing vain words of powers we cannot see,*
> *Blind divinations of a will supreme?*
> *Lost labour! when the circum-ambient gloom*
> *But holds, if gods, gods careless of our doom!*

He laid the book down with a sigh. It seemed to fit his case.

It was not until the next morning, however, that his anticipations were realised, and the telegraph messenger stopped at his door. The telegram was signed Eliphalet Hodges, and merely said, "Come at once. You are needed."

"Needed"! What could they "need" of him? "Wanted" would have been a better word,—"wanted" by the man who for sixteen years had forgotten that he had a son. He had already decided that he would not go, and was for the moment sorry that he had stayed where the telegram could reach him and stir his mind again into turmoil; but the struggle had already recommenced. Maybe his father was burdening his good old friends, and it was they who "needed" him. Then it was his duty to go, but not for his father's sake. He would not even see his father. No, not that! He could not see him.

It ended by his getting his things together and taking the next train. He was going, he told himself, to the relief of his guardian and his friend, and not because his father—his father!—wanted him. Did he deceive himself? Were there not, at the bottom of it all, the natural promptings of so close a relationship which not even cruelty, neglect, and degradation could wholly stifle?

He saw none of the scenes that had charmed his heart on the outward journey a few days before; for now his sight was either far ahead or entirely inward. When he reached Dexter, it was as if years had passed since he left its smoky little station. Things did not look familiar to him as he went up the old street, because he saw them with new eyes.

114

Mr. Hodges must have been watching for him, for he opened the door before he reached it.

"Come in, Freddie," he said in a low voice, tiptoeing back to his chair. "I've got great news fur you."

"You needn't tell me what it is," said Brent. "I know that my father is here."

Eliphalet started up. "Who told you?" he said; "some blockhead, I'll be bound, who didn't break it to you gently as I would 'a' done. Actu'lly the people in this here town—"

"Don't blame the people, Uncle 'Liph," said the young man, smiling in spite of himself. "I found it out for myself before I arrived; and, I assure you, it wasn't gently broken to me either." To the old man's look of bewildered amazement, Brent replied with the story of his meeting with his father.

"It's the good Lord's doin's," said Eliphalet, reverently.

"I don't know just whose doing it is, but it is an awful accusation to put on the Lord. I've still got enough respect for Him not to believe that."

"Freddie," exclaimed the old man, horror-stricken, "you ain't a-gettin' irreverent, you ain't a-beginnin' to doubt, air you? Don't do it. I know jest what you've had to bear all along, an' I know what you're a-bearin' now, but you ain't the only one that has their crosses. I'm a-bearin' my own, an' it ain't light neither. You don't know what it is, my boy, when you feel that somethin' precious is all your own, to have a real owner come in an' snatch it away from you. While I thought yore father was dead, you seemed like my own son; but now it 'pears like I 'ain't got no kind o' right to you an' it's kind o' hard, Freddie, it's kind o' hard, after all these years. I know how a mother feels when she loses her baby, but when it's a grown son that's lost, one that she's jest been pilin' up love fur, it's—it's—" The old man paused, overcome by his emotions.

"I am as much—no, more than ever your son, Uncle 'Liph. No one shall ever come between us; no, not even the man I should call father."

"He is yore father, Freddie. It's jest like I told Hester. She was fur sendin' him along." In spite of himself, a pang shot through Brent's heart at this. "But I said, 'No, no, Hester, he's Fred's father an' we must take him in, fur our boy's sake.'"

"Not for my sake, not for my sake!" broke out the young man.

"Well, then, fur our Master's sake. We took him in. He was

mighty low down. It seemed like the Lord had jest spared him to git here. Hester's with him now, an'—an'—kin you stand to hear it?—the doctor says he's only got a little while to live."

"Oh, I can stand it," Brent replied, with unconscious irony. The devotion and the goodness of the old man had softened him as thought, struggle, and prayer had failed to do.

"Will you go in now?" asked Eliphalet. "He wants to see you; he can't die in peace without."

The breath came hard between his teeth as Brent replied, "I said I wouldn't see him. I came because I thought you needed me."

"He's yore father, Freddie, an' he's penitent. All of us pore mortals need a good deal o' furgivin', an' it doesn't matter ef one of us needs a little more or a little less than another: it puts us all on the same level. Remember yore sermon about charity, an'—an' jedge not. You 'ain't seen all o' His plan. Come on." And, taking the young man by the hand, he led him into the room that had been his own. Hester rose as he entered, and shook hands with him, and then she and her husband silently passed out.

The sufferer lay upon the bed, his eyes closed and his face as white as the pillows on which he reclined. Disease had fattened on the hollow cheeks and wasted chest. One weak hand picked aimlessly at the coverlet, and the laboured breath caught and faltered as if already the hand of Death was at his throat.

The young man stood by the bed, trembling in every limb, his lips now as white as the ashen face before him. He was cold, but the perspiration stood in beads on his brow as he stood gazing upon the face of his father. Something like pity stirred him for a moment, but a vision of his own life came up before him, and his heart grew hard again. Here was the man who had wronged him irremediably.

Finally the dying man stirred uneasily, muttering, "I dreamed that he had come."

"I am here." Brent's voice sounded strange to him.

The eyes opened, and the sufferer gazed at him. "Are you—"

"I am your son."

"You—why, I—saw you—"

"You saw me in Cincinnati at the door of a beer-garden." He felt as if he had struck the man before him with a lash.

"Did—you—go in?"

"No: I went to your temperance meeting."

The elder Brent did not hear the ill-concealed bitterness in his son's voice. "Thank God," he said. "You heard—my—story, an'—it leaves me—less—to tell. Something—made me speak—to you that—night. Come nearer. Will—you—shake hands with—me?"

Fred reached over and took the clammy hand in his own.

"I have—had—a pore life," the now fast weakening man went on; "an' I have—done wrong—by—you, but I—have—repented. Will you forgive me?"

Something came up into Brent's heart and burned there like a flame.

"You have ruined my life," he answered, "and left me a heritage of shame and evil."

"I know it—God help me—I know it; but won't—you—forgive me, my son? I—want to—call you—that—just once." He pressed his hand closer.

Could he forgive him? Could he forget all that he had suffered and would yet suffer on this man's account? Then the words and the manner of old Eliphalet came to him, and he said, in a softened voice, "I forgive you, father." He hesitated long over the name.

"Thank God for—for—the name—an'—forgiveness." He carried his son's hand to his lips, "I sha'n't be—alive—long—now,—an' my—death—will set—people—to talkin'. They will—bring—up the—past. I—don't want you—to—stay an' have—to bear—it. I don't want to—bring any more on—you than I have—already. Go—away, as—soon as I am dead."

"I cannot leave my friends to bear my burdens."

"They will not speak—of them—as they—will speak of—you, my—poor—boy. You—are—old—Tom Brent's—son. I—wish I could take—my name—an' all—it means—along—with—me. But—promise—me—you—will—go. Promise—"

"I will go if you so wish it."

"Thank—you. An'—now—good-bye. I—can't talk—any—more. I don't dare—to advise—you—after—all—you—know—of me; but do—right—do right."

The hand relaxed and the eyelids closed. Brent thought that he was dead, and prompted by some impulse, bent down and kissed his father's brow,—his father, after all. A smile flitted over the pale face, but the eyes did not open. But he did not die then. Fred called Mrs. Hodges and left her with his father while he sat with Eliphalet. It was not until the next morning, when the air was full of sunlight, the song of birds, and the chime of church bells, that old Tom Brent's weary spirit passed out on its search for God. He had not spoken after his talk with his son.

There were heavy hearts about his bed, but there were no tears, no sorrow for his death,—only regret for the manner of his life.

Mrs. Hodges and Eliphalet agreed that the dead man had been right in wishing his son to go away, and, after doing what he could to lighten their load, he again stood on the threshold, leaving his old sad home. Mrs. Hodges bade him good-bye at the door, and went back. She was too bowed to seem hard any more, or even to pretend it. But Eliphalet followed him to the gate. The two stood holding each other's hands and gazing into each other's eyes.

"I know you're a-goin' to do right without me a-tellin' you to," said the old man, chokingly. "That's all I want of you. Even ef you don't preach, you kin live an' work fur Him."

"I shall do all the good I can, Uncle 'Liph, but I shall do it in the name of poor humanity until I come nearer to Him. I am dazed and confused now, and want the truth."

"Go on, my boy; you're safe. You've got the truth now, only you don't know it; fur they's One that says, 'Inasmuch as ye have done it unto one of the least of these, ye have done it unto me.'"

Another hearty hand-shake, and the young man was gone.

As Fred went down the street, some one accosted him and said, "I hear yore father's home."

"Yes, he's home," said Fred.

Tom Brent was buried on Tuesday morning. The Rev. Mr. Simpson, who, in spite of his age, had been prevailed upon to resume charge of his church, preached the sermon. He spoke feelingly of the "dear departed brother, who, though late, had found acceptance with the Lord," and he ended with a prayer—which was a shot—for the "departed's misguided son, who had rejected his Master's call and was now wandering over the earth in rebellion and sin." It was well that he did not see the face of Eliphalet Hodges then.

Dan'l Hastings nodded over the sermon. In the back part of the church, Mrs. Martin and Mrs. Smith whispered together and gaped at the two old mourners, and wondered where the boy was. They had "heerd he was in town."

Bill Tompkins brought Elizabeth to the funeral.

CHAPTER XVII

I n another town than Dexter the events narrated in the last chapter would have proved a nine days' wonder, gained their meed of golden gossip, and then given way to some newer sensation. But not so here. This little town was not so prolific in startling episodes that she could afford to let such a one pass with anything less than the fullest comment. The sudden return of Tom Brent, his changed life, and his death were talked of for many a day. The narrative of his life was yet to be a stock camp-meeting sermon story, and the next generation of Dexterites was destined to hear of him. He became a part of the town's municipal history.

Fred's disappearance elicited no less remark. Speculations as to his whereabouts and his movements were rife. The storm of gossip which was going on around them was not lost on Eliphalet Hodges and his wife. But, save when some too adventurous inquirer called down upon himself Mrs. Hodges' crushing rebuke or the old man's mild resentment, they went their ways silent and uncommunicative.

They had heard from the young man first about two weeks after his departure. He had simply told them that he had got a place in the office of a packing establishment. Furthermore, he had begged that they let his former fellow-townsmen know nothing of his doings or of his whereabouts, and the two old people had religiously respected his wishes. Perhaps there was some reluctance on the part of Mrs. Hodges, for after the first letter she said, "It does seem like a sin an' a shame, 'Liphalet, that we can't tell these here people how nice Fred's a-doin', so's to let 'em know that he don't need none o' their help. It jest makes my tongue fairly itch when I see Mis' Smith an' that bosom crony o' her'n, Sallie Martin, a-nosin' around tryin' to see what they kin find out."

"It is amazin' pesterin', Hester. I'm su'prised at how I feel about it myself, fur I never was no hand to want to gossip; but when I hear old Dan'l Hastings, that can't move out o' his cheer fur the rheumatiz,—when I hear him a-sayin' that he reckoned that Fred was a-goin' to the dogs, I felt jest like up an' tellin' him how things was."

"Why on airth didn't you? Ef I'd 'a' been there, I 'd—"

"But you know what Freddie's letter said. I kept still on that account; but I tell you I looked at Dan'l." From his pocket the old man took the missive worn with many readings, and gazed at it fondly. "Yes," he repeated, "I looked at Dan'l hard. I felt jest like up an' tellin' him."

"Well, no wonder. I'm afeared I'd 'a' clean furgot Freddie's wishes an' told him everything. To think of old Dan'l Hastings, as old he is, a-gossipin' about other people's business! Sakes alive! he needs every breath he's got now fur his prayers,—as all of us pore mortals do now," added Mrs. Hodges, as she let her eyes fall upon her own wrinkled hands.

"Yes, we're old, Hester, you an' I; but I'm mighty glad o' the faith I've been a-storin' up, fur it's purty considerable of a help now."

"Of course, 'Liphalet, faith is a great comfort, but it's a greater one to know that you've allus tried to do yore dooty the very best you could; not a-sayin' that you 'ain't tried."

"Most of us tries, Hester, even Dan'l."

"I ain't a-goin' to talk about Dan'l Hastings. He's jest naturally spiteful an' crabbed. I declare, I don't see how he's a-goin' to squeeze into the kingdom."

"Oh, never mind that, Hester. God ain't a-goin' to ask you to find a way."

Mrs. Hodges did not reply. She and her husband seldom disagreed now, because he seldom contradicted or found fault with her. But if this dictum of his went unchallenged, it was not so with some later conclusions at which he arrived on the basis of another of Fred's letters.

It was received several months after the settlement of the young man in Cincinnati, and succeeded a long silence. "You will think," it ran, "that I have forgotten you; but it is not so. My life has been very full here of late, it is true, but not so full as to exclude you and good Aunt Hester. I feel that I am growing. I can take good full breaths here. I couldn't in Dexter: the air was too rarefied by religion."

Mrs. Hodges gasped as her husband read this aloud, but there was the suspicion of a smile about the corners of Eliphalet's mouth.

"You ask me if I attend any church," the letter went on. "Yes, I do. When I first left, I thought that I never wanted to see the inside of a meeting-house again. But there is a young lady in our office who is very much interested in church work, and somehow she has got me interested too, and I go to her church every Sunday. It is Congregational."

"Congregational!" exclaimed Mrs. Hodges. "Congregational! an' he borned an' raised up in the Methodist faith. It's the first step."

"He wasn't borned nothin' but jest a pore little outcast sinner, an' as fur as the denomination goes, I guess that church is about as good as any other."

"'Liphalet Hodges, air you a-backslidin' too?"

"No: I'm like Freddie; I'm a-growin'."

"It's a purty time of life fur you to be a-talkin' about growin'. You're jest like an old tree that has fell in a damp place an' sen's out a few shoots on the trunk. It thinks it's a-growin' too, but them shoots soon wither, an' the tree rots; that's what it does."

"But before it rotted, it growed all that was in it to grow, didn't it. Well, that's all anybody kin do, tree or human bein'." He paused for a moment. "I 'ain't got all my growth yit."

"You kin git the rest in the garden of the Lord."

"It ain't good to change soil on some plants too soon. I ain't ready to be set out." He went on reading:

"'I'm not so narrow as I was at home. I don't think so many things are wrong as I used to. It is good to be like other people sometimes, and not to feel yoreself apart from all the rest of humanity. I am growing to act more like the people I meet, and so I am—'" the old man's hand trembled, and he moved the paper nearer to his eyes—"'I—' What's this he says? 'I am learning to dance.'"

"There!" his wife shot forth triumphantly. "What did I tell you? Going to a Congregational church an' learnin' to dance, an' he not a year ago a preacher of the gospel."

Eliphalet was silent for some time: his eyes looked far out into space. Then he picked up the paper that had fluttered from his hand, and a smile flitted over his face.

"Well, I don't know," he said. "Freddie's young, an' they's worse things in the world than dancin'."

"You ain't a-upholdin' him in that too, air you? Well, I never! You'd uphold that sinful boy ef he committed murder."

"I ain't a-upholdin' nothin' but what I think is right."

"Right! 'Liphalet Hodges, what air you a-sayin'?"

"Not that I mean to say that dancin' is right, but—"

"There ain't no 'buts' in the Christian religion, 'Liphalet, an' there ain't no use in yore tryin' to cover up Freddie's faults."

"I ain't a-tryin' to cover nothin' up from God. But sometimes I git to thinkin' that mebbe we put a good many more bonds on ourselves than the Lord ever meant us to carry."

"Oh, some of us don't struggle under none too heavy burdens. Some of us have a way of jest slippin' 'em off of our shoulders like a bag of flour."

"Meanin' me. Well, mebbe I have tried to make things jest as easy fur myself as possible, but I 'ain't never tried to make 'em no harder fur other people. I like to think of the Master as a good gentle friend, an' mebbe I 'ain't shifted so many o' the burdens He put on me that He won't let me in at last."

"'Liphalet, I didn't say what I said fur no slur ag'in' you. You're as good a Christian man as—well, as most."

"I know you didn't mean no slur, Hester. It was jest yore dooty to say it. I've come to realise how strong yore feelin' about dooty is, in the years we've been together, an' I wouldn't want you to be any different."

The calm of old age had come to these two. Life's turbulent waters toss us and threaten to rend our frail bark in pieces. But the swelling of the tempest only lifts us higher, and finally we reach and rest upon the Ararat of age, with the swirling floods below us.

Eliphalet went on with the letter. "He says some more about that little girl. 'Alice is a very nice and sensible girl. I like her very much. She helps me to get out of myself and to be happy. I have never known before what a good thing it was to be happy,—perhaps because I have tried so hard to be so. I believe that I have been selfish and egotistical.' Freddie don't furgit his words," the old man paused to say. "'I have always thought too much of myself, and not enough of others. That was the reason that I was not strong enough to live down the opposition in Dexter. It seems that, after all your kindness to me, I might have stayed and made you and Aunt Hester happy for the rest of your days.' Bless that boy! 'But the air stifled me. I could not breathe in it. Now that I am away, I can look back and see it all—my mistakes and my shortcomings; for my horizon is broader and I can see clearer. I have learned to know what pleasure is, and it has been like a stimulant to me. I have been given a greater chance to love, and it has been like the breath of life to me. I have come face to face with Christianity without cant, and I respect it for what it is. Alice understands me and brings out the best that is in me. I have always thought that it was good for a young man to have a girl friend.'"

For an instant, Mrs. Hodges resumed her old manner. A slight wave from the old flood had reached the bark and rocked it. She pursed her lips and shook her head. "He furgot Elizabeth in a mighty short time."

"Ef he hadn't he'd ought to be spanked like a child. Elizabeth never was the kind of a mate fur Freddie, an' there ain't nobody that knows it better than you yoreself, Hester, an' you know it."

Mrs. Hodges did not reply. The wavelet had subsided again.

"Now jest listen how he ends up. 'I want you and Aunt Hester to come down and see me when you can. I will send for you in a week or two, if you will promise to come. Write to me, both of you. Won't you? Your changed boy, Fred.' Changed, an' I'm glad of it. He's more like a natural boy of his age now than he ever was before. He's jest like a young oak saplin'. Before he allus put me in mind o' one o' them oleander slips that you used to cut off an' hang ag'in' the house in a bottle o' water so's they'd root. We'll go down, won't we, Hester? We'll go down, an' see him."

"Not me, 'Liphalet. You kin go; but I ain't a-goin' nowhere to be run over by the cars or wrecked or somethin'. Not that I'm so powerful afeared of anything like that, fur I do hope I'm prepared to go whenever the Master calls; but it ain't fur me to begin a-runnin' around at my age, after livin' all these years at home. No, indeed. Why, I couldn't sleep in no other bed but my own now. I don't take to no sich new things."

And go Mrs. Hodges would not. So Eliphalet was forced to write and refuse the offered treat. But on a day there came another letter, and he could no longer refuse to grant the wish of his beloved boy. The missive was very brief. It said only, "Alice has promised to marry me. Won't you and Aunt Hester come and see me joined to the dearest girl in the world?" There was a postscript to it: "I did not love Elizabeth. I know it now."

"Hester, I'm a-goin'." said Eliphalet.

"Go on, 'Liphalet, go on. I want you to go, but I'm set in my ways now. I do hope that girl kin do something besides work in an office. She ought to be a good housekeeper, an' a good cook, so's not to kill that pore child with dyspepsy. I do hope she won't put saleratus in her biscuits."

"I think it's Freddie's soul that needs feedin.'"

"His soul'll go where it don't need feedin', ef his stomach ain't 'tended to right. Ef I went down there, I could give the girl some points."

"I don't reckon you'd better go, Hester. As you say, you're set in yore ways, an' mebbe her ways 'ud be diff'rent; an' then—then you'd both feel it."

"Oh, I suppose she thinks she knows it all, like most young people do."

"I hope she don't; but I'm a-goin' down to see her anyhow, an' I'll carry yore blessin' along with mine."

For the next week, great were the preparations for the old man's departure, and when finally he left the old gate and turned his back on the little cottage it was as if he were going on a great journey rather than a trip of less than a hundred miles. It had been a long time since he had been on a train, and at first he felt a little dubious. But he was soon at home, for his kindly face drew his fellow-passengers to him, and he had no lack of pleasant companions on the way.

Like Fred, the noises of the great station would have bewildered him, but as he alighted and passed through the gate a strong hand was laid on his shoulder, and his palm was pressing the palm of his beloved son. The old carpet-bag fell from his hands.

"Freddie Brent, it ain't you?"

"It's I, Uncle 'Liph, and no one else. And I'm so glad to see you that I don't know what to do. Give me that bag."

They started away, the old man chattering like a happy child. He could not keep from feasting his eyes on the young man's face and form.

"Well, Freddie, you jest don't look like yoreself. You're— you're—"

"I'm a man, Uncle 'Liph."

"I allus knowed you'd be, my boy. I allus knowed you'd be. But yore aunt Hester told me to ask you ef—ef you'd dropped all yore religion. She's mighty disturbed about yore dancin'."

Brent laughed aloud in pure joy.

"I knowed you hadn't," the old man chuckled.

"Lost it all? Uncle 'Liph, why, I've just come to know what religion is. It's to get bigger and broader and kinder, and to live and to love and be happy, so that people around you will be happy."

"You're still a first-rate preacher, Freddie."

"Oh, yes, Uncle 'Liph; I've been to a better school than the Bible Seminary. I haven't got many religious rules and formulas, but I'm trying to live straight and do what is right."

The old man had paused with tears in his eyes. "I been a-prayin' fur you," he said.

"So has Alice," replied the young man, "though I don't see why she needs to pray. She's a prayer in herself. She has made me better by letting me love her. Come up, Uncle 'Liph. I want you to see her before we go on to my little place."

They stopped before a quiet cottage, and Fred knocked. In the little parlour a girl came to them. She was little, not quite up to Fred's shoulder. His eyes shone as he looked down upon her brown head. There were lines about her mouth, as if she had known sorrow that had blossomed into sweetness. The young man took her hand. "Uncle 'Liph," he said, "this is Alice."

She came forward with winning frankness, and took the old man's hand in hers. The tears stood in his eyes again.

"This is Alice," he said; "this is Alice." Then his gaze travelled to Fred's glowing face, and, with a sob in his voice that was all for joy, he added, "Alice, I'm glad you're a-livin'."

THE END

Paul Laurence Dunbar (1872-1906) was born in Dayton, Ohio, where he attended high school as the only African-American enrolled. A gifted student, he was president of his class, as well as editor of the school newspaper and president of the literary society. He started writing poetry as a young child, and it was in that field where he gained his principal place in American literature. Dunbar was, in fact, the first African-American to gain significant acceptance as a poet.

In 1898, he married poet Alice Ruth Moore, but their relationship was stormy, partly because of his growing dependence on alcohol (beginning when his doctor urged him to drink in order to find relief from his tuberculosis).

Dunbar was associated with some of the most important and famous people of his time, including his former classmates and lifelong friends Orville and Wilbur Wright and the two most prominent African-Americans then living—Frederick Douglass and Booker T. Washington. In addition, he received a ceremonial sword from President Theodore Roosevelt.

The works of Paul Laurence Dunbar include numerous volumes of poetry and five novels. His ill-health, however, led to an early death at the age of thirty-three.

Made in the USA
San Bernardino, CA
27 December 2017